THE FORTUNES OF TEXAS

Follow the lives and loves of a complex family with a rich history and deep ties in the Lone Star State

FORTUNE'S FAMILY SECRETS

With Archibald Fortune's death comes the revelation of a stunning secret: The Emerald Ridge scion had three separate families and one child he'd always longed to find! Can his shocked children come together to find Archibald's missing heir and claim the family inheritance—or will strife tear them apart?

FORTUNE'S PRICELESS COWBOY

Jillian Fortune's on a mission: To find out why her late father would have bequeathed land to a mysterious sibling who must be found. Key to that mystery? Cowboy Nick Slater, ranch caretaker and devoted uncle to the orphaned little girl he's raising as his own. The last thing he needs is a complication like Jillian. But as Nick helps untangle her father's deception, maybe it's his good fortune to find *exactly* what his shuttered heart needs most—Jillian herself!

Dear Reader,

Welcome (or welcome back!) to Emerald Ridge, Texas, a charming town filled with big-city glitz, country glam and a whole lot of secrets. In this story, I'm so excited to take you back to the Fortune and Daughters Ranch, home to a stable filled with rare horses, a brooding cowboy and an heiress looking for answers. Not to mention the backdrop for new love!

When a misunderstanding-at-first-sight pulls Jillian Fortune and Nick Slater together, a reluctant partnership blossoms into something beautiful between them. While Jillian searches for her place in the world, Nick yearns to be comfortable in his, and together they find the support they both need to succeed.

I've always believed that the right people come along when we need them most in life. All we have to do is open ourselves up to the potential of new possibilities. So here's to everyone still looking for their place or their person or their purpose! I can't wait for you to dive into this happily-ever-after in my first Fortunes of Texas story, and I hope Jillian and Nick's journey brings you both some inspiration and some comfort. If swooning over sexy cowboys or chatting books is your thing, you can find me on Instagram @elizabethhrib or at elizabethhrib.com.

Elizabeth

FORTUNE'S PRICELESS COWBOY

ELIZABETH HRIB

THE FORTUNES OF TEXAS

Special thanks and acknowledgment are given to Elizabeth Hrib for her contribution to The Fortunes of Texas: Fortune's Family Secrets miniseries.

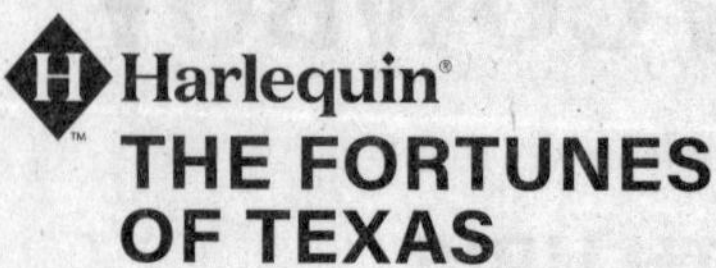

Recycling programs for this product may not exist in your area.

ISBN-13: 978-1-335-14332-7

Fortune's Priceless Cowboy

Harlequin Enterprises ULC
22 Adelaide St. West, 41st Floor
Toronto, Ontario M5H 4E3, Canada
www.Harlequin.com

HarperCollins Publishers
Macken House, 39/40 Mayor Street Upper,
Dublin 1, D01 C9W8, Ireland
www.HarperCollins.com

Printed in Lithuania

Elizabeth Hrib was born and raised in London, Ontario, where she spends her nine-to-five as a nurse. She fell in love with the romance genre while bingeing '90s rom-coms. When she's not nursing or writing, she can be found at the piano, swooning over her favorite books on Instagram or buying too many houseplants.

Books by Elizabeth Hrib

Fortunes of Texas: Fortune's Family Secrets

Fortune's Priceless Cowboy

Montana Mavericks: The Tenacity Social Club

All In with the Maverick

Harlequin Special Edition

Hatchet Lake

Lightning Strikes Twice
Flirting with Disaster

Visit the Author Profile page at Harlequin.com for more titles.

Chapter One

Jillian Fortune had always been a horse girl—a label she'd wear loud and proud for the rest of her life. Sure, she liked her Louboutins and her Stella maxi dresses and her Chanel No. 5. What woman didn't? But she'd never shied away from the overwhelming smell of the stables, all sweat and fur and earthiness, or mucking out a stall or grooming her horse after a rough, muddy gallop through the rain.

For all intents and purposes, the stables at the Fortune and Daughters Ranch were her favorite place in the world. Or, they *had* been, once upon a time. Now she hesitated walking through these doors, just as she had for the past month.

Ever since learning that her dad had passed away, suffering a sudden heart attack on a business trip to New York City, the stables had felt different. It wasn't an unwelcoming feeling, per se, but there was a weight that accompanied her here now—a constant reminder that Archibald was gone—and Jillian was still struggling with how to feel about that. Despite breaking down in tears when her dad's attorney had delivered the news, she was still trying to reconcile how to miss someone who'd spent his entire life lying to her.

Jillian knuckled a spot in her chest, rubbing at the ache that throbbed every time she replayed that horrible day.

A horse whinnied, long and loud, probably demanding attention, and she was pulled from her thoughts briefly, a small smile curving her lips. The rare horses housed in the stables had all belonged to her dad—every one of them cared for by a dedicated team of stable hands. Now, looking back over his life, Jillian truly believed that the horses were an indulgence her dad had allowed himself. He may have run a billion-dollar airline, but Archibald Fortune had never been one for material possessions. The horses though… His love for the beautiful animals was one of the few things she had genuinely shared in common with him. That fact made her breath catch now, and she let out a heavy sigh as she forced herself through the doors.

One step.

Then another.

Inside, the coiling tension in her chest eased as the scents of hay and leather and oats washed over her. It smelled like home, like *comfort*, and Jillian made a promise to herself—the same promise she'd been making for weeks—not to let her dad's death chase her from this place that brought her so much joy.

She stuffed her hands in the pockets of her vest, leaning her head back, face turned toward the massive wooden beams that stretched to the rafters of the peaked building.

Inhale.

Exhale.

Everything was going to be okay. Settled, she slowly made her way down the center aisle between the horse stalls. The cement floors were lined with rich, golden straw. Sunlight filtered in through high windows, catching glossy coats as the horses shifted, their heads bent in their feed buckets. Her dad had amassed quite the collection over the years: an Akhal-Teke from Turkmenistan with its shimmering silvery coat, a Marwari from India with its unique, inward-curving ears, a small Caspian—one of the first horse breeds Jillian had learned to ride on—and several white Camargues. There was also a Gypsy Vanner with its feathered legs, and three Andalusian horses that had arrived only a few months ago. Had Archibald even had a chance to enjoy them before he—

Jillian struggled to fight off that thought. She often wondered what her dad had been thinking about before he died. His family? *Families?* Maybe he hadn't had time to think about anything at all. Widowmaker—that was what the doctors had called the heart attack that killed him. And it certainly had made a widow out of… Well, all three of his wives.

A gate rattled ahead, and Jillian blinked away the weight behind her eyes, smiling as she spotted her favorite horse of the bunch. He was a gentle, all-black Friesian named King, and she'd doted on him since the moment he'd arrived. If there were shampoo commercials for horses, King would star in every single one of them, showing off his long flowing mane and tail. He was the Fabio of horses, and catching sight of him out in the pasture, with the sun on his coat, was always a breathtaking sight.

Jillian was sure to remind him he was a beautiful boy every chance she got.

"Howdy, Ms. Fortune," a young man drawled as he passed in a hurry, a saddle thrown over his shoulder. He dipped his head briefly before rushing off.

"Good mornin', Ms. Fortune," another greeted. He led one of the Andalusians by the reins, a bristled brush in his hand.

"Morning," she said, giving them both a tight smile. She knew their names. Probably. Somewhere in the back of her mind. They'd just escaped her at the moment. Or maybe she'd never known them, which wasn't inconceivable. She felt like the stable hands switched over so often it was hard to remember who was coming and going, and she usually tried to stay out of their way when they were working, preferring the quiet times in-between feeds to be alone in here with her thoughts. Plus, it had been a long time since she'd actually required anyone's help to saddle her horse. She'd been managing her own tack since she was a young girl.

People often thought her slight and delicate and far too girly to get her hands dirty, but when it came to the horses, Jillian was as strong and capable as any seasoned cowboy. She made her way to King's stall, greeting her black beauty by leaning over the gate and offering him a rub on the forelock. He came to her without hesitation, tossing his head up and down as if to say hello.

"Hi there, beautiful boy," she said as he nuzzled at her, bumping her face with his massive one before snuffling at her puffy vest. She knew he wanted in her pockets. He was always looking for treats. She laughed. "Not even a hello first?"

King made a chuffing noise, and Jillian stepped back to unzip her vest. She was too warm anyway with her long-sleeve thermal underneath. February had turned to March, bringing with it warmer weather, though most days Jillian still felt trapped in that cold, endless loop of bad news that had started the day her entire life flipped upside down. When she closed her eyes, she could still see the lawyer standing there in the living room of the main house, reading out the letter her dad had left for them in the unfortunate event of his death. The words turned over and over in her mind.

Above all else: I am deeply sorry for the heartache this will cause all of you. I have three separate families. Three wives, with whom I have five children—Shelby and Jillian, Hayes and Penn, and Madeline. I have kept you all a secret from one another.

Jillian still couldn't believe it. Some days she woke up thinking it was all a fever dream, then she'd walk downstairs, see the look of grief on her mother's face and remember that, yes, her dad had been a bigamist, dropping this bombshell on them all when he was no longer around to have to deal with it. But not only had her absentee father left three families behind, he'd also revealed that he'd had an affair in Emerald Ridge thirty years ago with a woman named Lianna Dunhill. She'd apparently gotten pregnant, and, when her dad had refused to marry her, uncovered his secrets and blackmailed him. After paying her off with millions, she'd disappeared from his life, but here was the real kicker her dad had left in his letter:

> I am leaving my vast fortune to be split equally among my three families with one caveat… For my children to inherit my fortune, I require that all five of you work together to find your missing sibling. Upon confirmation of DNA testing, this heir will then inherit a particular parcel of very valuable land in Emerald Ridge that holds the key to my past and may help you all find peace with who your father was.

So now, at twenty-nine, Jillian had inherited three brand new adult siblings—Madeline, Hayes and Penn—and a potential missing fourth. And the only way any of them were getting their inheritance was to track down this missing sibling. Without the help of her father's money, Jillian had no idea if she would be able to keep the stables running. She had some savings from the monthly allowance her father had provided, but nowhere near enough to maintain all the expert care and training the horses required long term. On top of that, her biological sister, Shelby, was now almost six months pregnant and planning a wedding.

Jillian was about to be an aunt and a maid of honor, and she still had no idea what the hell she was supposed to be doing with her own life in the wake of this mess. To say she was stressed was an understatement, but the only way forward was…well…*forward.*

King chuffed again, impatient. *At least some things never change*, she thought as she produced a bright red apple from her pocket. "Is this what you're looking for?"

He nickered at the sight.

"You'd never lie to me, would you?" Jillian said as she held the treat out for him in the palm of her hand. "Because you're a good boy." She rubbed his forelock again. "Dependable, uncomplicated…trustworthy." How did she have more faith in a horse than she'd had in her own dad?

King's ears twitched as he munched on the apple, the crunch satisfying as the treat quickly disappeared. While the horse enjoyed that, Jillian pulled out her phone and texted the group chat that consisted of her two best friends, Melissa and Rory.

Phase one of "find the missing sibling" is a go! she wrote.

Melissa sent back a surprised face emoji. You're meeting the mysterious caretaker today?

Any minute now, Jillian texted back. We agreed to meet in the stables at nine. Madeline Fortune, her new half sister, had been doing some research into the parcel of valuable land their dad intended to leave his potential sixth heir. Apparently, it was located on the other side of Emerald Ridge, past the downtown core near the railroad tracks. Not only had she found the land but also the caretaker: a man named Nick Slater. As it turned out, Nick was one of the four cowboys that cared for their dad's rare horses on the ranch; so, in a show of teamwork with her siblings—one of the conditions of her dad's will—she'd offered to meet with Nick since she was conveniently already living on the property.

Ooo, keep us posted, Melissa wrote.

Yes, we want to hear everything! Rory chimed in. The girls had been her rock since her dad had passed and everything that transpired with the reading of his will. They'd been supportive and nonjudgmental, letting Jillian vent and cry until she'd exhausted herself, and then they'd taken her out for drinks so they could spitball theories about Lianna Dunhill and the mysterious heir that might or might not exist. With Shelby so wrapped up in her pregnancy and her new fiancé, Jillian was grateful to have the girls in her corner. She wasn't sure what she would have done without them this past month.

Jillian sent a thumbs-up. Meet up after at Coffee Connection?

Yes! Melissa and Rory typed almost simultaneously. The café was one of their favorite places to debrief, with its large, overstuffed chairs and cozy atmosphere. Plus, by the time this was all said and done, Jillian was definitely going to need some caffeine. Because what Jillian wanted to understand most of all was why some random cowboy had been selected to care for a piece of land that obviously meant a lot to her dad.

Why Nick?

What was so special about him that her dad had entrusted him with the task? Archibald wasn't one to forge personal connections, not even with his own kids.

Jillian released a breath that rattled her lips together. Honestly, the last thing she wanted to do was dig into this mess. In her experience, wanting to know her dad, wanting to bond with him, had only ever hurt her. There was less disappointment in life if you just walled off your heart and kept people at a distance.

King nuzzled at her again, looking for another apple as Jillian stuffed her phone away. She was doing this for him, she reminded herself. For all the horses that she loved so much. And for her family, who deserved some kind of closure. Whatever the heck that looked like.

"That's all I had," she laughed, giving him a soft pat. "Don't be greedy."

"Are you a princess?" a small voice said, startling Jillian.

She whirled around, caught off guard by the question, but even more surprised to find a tiny girl looking up at her. Her blond hair had been pulled into lopsided pigtails with two different colored hair ties, and she had the bluest eyes Jillian had ever seen. She couldn't be more than four, and she was positively adorable.

"Hi, sweetie," Jillian said, glancing around. Since when did they have children this young in the stables? Where had she come from?

The girl lifted her finger, pointing up at Jillian. "You a *princess*?"

"What was that?" she asked, still scanning the aisle for the child's parent. Jillian put her hand on the girl's shoulder to keep her from running off. The horses were all penned or out in the pasture, but there were still a lot of nooks and crannies a tiny girl could disappear into. Places she probably shouldn't be.

"Princess," the girl repeated, her voice no more than a whisper now.

Jillian looked down at her. She didn't know whether to laugh or not. "Umm… No, sweetie. Sorry."

But aren't *you*? a deep voice rumbled. Or, at least, that was what Jillian thought before reminding herself what a ridiculous thing that would actually be to say. Jillian watched a man stride toward them, his cowboy boots kicking up dust, and her mouth went a little dry. He was tall, with dark brown hair and enough swagger to draw every eye in the room. Even the horses seemed to take note of him. Jillian tilted her head, giving him a long up-and-down look. *Heavens!* She was being far too obvious, but she couldn't help herself. The man was a walking ad for Stetsons and fitted blue jeans.

"Mandy, I told you not to run off in the stables," he said. The little girl gave him a shy smile, pointing up at King. The man shook his head. "Don't think a distraction is going to work, Squeaks."

Jillian smiled at the adorable nickname.

"Hope she didn't cause you any trouble," the man murmured, glancing up at her.

"Not at all." Jillian watched the corner of his mouth curl into a smile. Her breath caught in her throat. If she had thought the little girl had blue eyes, then his were…something else entirely. The man was striking, really. There was no other way to say it. He was clean-shaven, with a jaw that could cut steel and a perfect chin dimple. Jillian looked over the handsome cowboy once more and whoa, whoa, *whoa*! Hold on a second! Had she really just thought… *Handsome?*

She blinked repeatedly, dragging herself back to reality. Okay, objectively speaking, she supposed he *was* handsome. Ridiculously so. Though cowboy wasn't the kind of guy she usually went for. She was more interested in the buttoned-up, tailored-suit kind of guy. The type that spent weekends at charity galas and had a corner office carved out in the family business. At least, those were the kinds of guys that ran in her social circles. But maybe she needed to branch out more, because this rugged cowboy schtick was sort of doing something to her.

"She's adorable," Jillian continued.

"And she knows it," he said, holding his hand out. "I'm Nick Slater."

Jillian's eyes widened in surprise. "Oh? *Oh!*"

"Here for our meeting."

"Yes." How had she not made the connection? "Hi! Thanks for agreeing to speak with me."

"Hope it's okay I brought my niece." He gestured down to the girl. "Story hour at the library was cancelled at the last minute."

The little girl beamed up at her with that shy, tiny smile. "Perfectly okay," Jillian said. "Rotten luck with story time."

"Don't I know it," Nick said. "I had to promise ice cream later to make up for it."

"Sprinkles," the little girl whispered.

"With sprinkles," Nick confirmed, making Jillian chuckle. He gestured to the meeting space off to the left of the tack room. "Figured we could talk through here. There's a desk where Mandy can sit and color."

Jillian watched him stroll past, leading Mandy by the hand, and it took everything in her not to turn around and check out his backside. Melissa and Rory would be disappointed. As if they'd sensed her error, Jillian's phone buzzed, a message from Melissa popping up.

Sooooooo, what did you find out? Any secret land updates?

Jillian made sure Nick was nowhere near before replying. Just out of curiosity, how do we feel about cowboys?

What kind are we talking about? Rory wrote. Rough and tough, ready for a roll in the hay?

Or the smarmy, smooth-talking, hey-there-little-lady sort? Melissa added.

Jillian doubted Nick was the hey-there-little-lady type, but honestly, what did she really know about him? And that was exactly the reason she was here in the first place—to figure out who Nick Slater was and what he could tell her about the land and her dad. Because if she couldn't get more information out of him, she'd never track down this missing sibling, and then she might as well slap a "For Sale" sign on her beloved stables right now.

Not sure yet, she fired back quickly. I'll keep you posted.

Chapter Two

"Get on up here, Squeaks," Nick called to Mandy, pulling out a chair at the large table as Jillian followed him through the door of the meeting room. She closed it behind her with a soft thud.

Mandy skipped over to his side, smiling at her, and Jillian found herself smiling back. She'd always been good with kids, and she sometimes thought it was a shame that she'd been the youngest child. She could have done with a younger brother or sister to dote on. Then again, apparently her dad had run around giving her all sorts of siblings; she'd just not known about them until recently.

She flicked the lights on for Mandy, but that was probably unnecessary. Sunlight spilled in through two massive windows that looked out onto the round paddock at the side of the stables. The circular enclosure was usually used for training the horses. It was currently empty, but tracks were caked into the mud where specialized equine trainers often took the horses through their lunging and groundwork exercises. Beyond that, she could glimpse some of the pastures, the distant forms of grazing horses visible. As a young child, Jillian had spent hours in this room, watching the horses trot past while she did her homework. It was the second best thing to being out in the paddock herself or out riding. When she'd gotten older, and had been sent away to boarding school with Shelby, she'd spent her summers here, ducking out of the Texas heat in between lessons if her dad wasn't using the room for some business meeting or another.

Now it wouldn't get much use, she supposed, watching as Mandy climbed into the chair at the table where Jillian had once practiced her multiplication and fractions. Nick had come prepared with a coloring book and crayons, and the little girl's eyes lit up as she flipped the book open, immediately settling on a page with a fairytale kingdom and characters wearing crowns.

"I take it that princesses are a big thing in your world?" Jillian said, a teasing lilt to her voice.

"Princesses. Mermaids. Unicorns." Nick glanced up at her. "There's a hierarchy that must be respected."

Jillian chuckled, trying and failing not to be distracted by the dimples in his cheeks. "I see."

"Do you want to listen to your favorite story?" Nick asked Mandy. She took her time answering, instead focusing intently on selecting her first crayon—a bright pink—only to immediately scribble all over the page with vigor. It was as adorable as it was funny.

"Squeaks," Nick said, getting her attention again. "Story?"

She finally nodded.

Nick produced a pair of small, wireless headphones from the bag he'd brought, sliding them over Mandy's head, gently scooping her little blond baby hairs out of the way so they didn't get snagged. For such a big, burly guy, he was surprisingly gentle. Maybe that was how he'd ended up working with her dad's prized horses in the first place.

Rough and tough, ready for a roll in the hay...

Jillian's stomach flipped as she thought of Rory's message. He was a little of that too—rough and tough—judging by those broad shoulders. She startled herself with that thought. She needed to get her head on straight. Her mind could *not* be straying to such things. She was here about her dad and the land. Nothing more.

Once the headphones were adjusted over Mandy's ears, she frowned up at Nick and tugged on his pant leg. Jillian noted that the girl hadn't actually said anything since her initial princess and sprinkles comments, which struck her as odd for a kid of Mandy's age. Jillian wasn't an expert on preschoolers, but she *did* spend a lot of time volunteering in the children's department of the Emerald Ridge Memorial Hospital. And when those kids got talking, it was impossible to get them to stop. But Mandy seemed to have transitioned into communicating with gestures and facial expressions and pointing at her uncle.

It was definitely…*odd.*

"Give me a second," Nick laughed, pulling out his phone. He glanced over at Jillian. "We're making our way through *Princess Willow and the Enchanted Kingdom*."

"Sounds riveting," Jillian said.

"Personally, I'd rather a swift kick from a horse," Nick muttered under his breath. He waved his hand in front of Mandy's face. "Good?"

She nodded her head and silently mouthed the words to the story as she set to work again, scribbling over her scribbles in a new color. The drawing was very…abstract. Once Mandy was happily occupied and Nick had contained the crayons that were rolling off the table, Jillian cleared her throat.

"Guess we should get down to business?" he said.

Jillian nodded. Nick looked right at her, and she tried

not to be dazzled by those blue eyes again, but they were so riveting, she didn't know how she was ever supposed to look away.

"What did you want to talk about?" he prompted when she didn't say anything.

Jillian came back to her senses. "Oh, well… I was hoping to get some information on the land that my dad had out near the railroad tracks. And I've recently come to learn that you're the guy he hired to care for the land."

"Is something wrong?" Nick asked, frowning. "With the land, I mean?"

"Nothing's wrong," she assured him. "My family is just trying to…" How did she put this delicately? *Fulfill the terms of my dad's will so everyone gets their inheritance? Unearth the secrets he left behind? Maybe find yet another sibling?* "…come to terms with some of the things my dad left behind."

"Right," he said. "Well, I'll try to answer whatever I can."

"How long have you been working at the Fortune and Daughters Ranch?" Jillian asked.

Nick arched a thick eyebrow. His expression could only be described as perplexed. She didn't know what was so confusing about that question. "You're kidding, right?" he scoffed.

Jillian was a little taken aback by his tone. "I don't… I don't understand."

"Why are you asking that question like you have no idea who I am?" Nick said.

Now Jillian was the one who was confused. If she'd already known who he was, she wouldn't be in here, interviewing him. "I, well… We've never actually been introduced before, have we?"

"No, but you must have seen me around the ranch?"

She lifted her shoulder.

Nick crossed his arms, his eyes narrowing. Why was he looking at her like that? Was that…disdain? "You've really never seen me around before?" he clarified. "Or my niece?"

"I mean…maybe," she said.

He snorted. "*Maybe?*"

"Probably!" She tried to stay out of their employees' way in the mornings and afternoons when the horses were being tended to! It wasn't like it was her job to stand around the stables and oversee the staff. If anyone had done that, it would have been her dad. But the way Nick was looking at her now… She felt like she'd given the wrong answer. She was being judged. Harshly. Unfairly. For literally no reason! Jillian bristled. "Look, as I mentioned, my dad died last month. I haven't exactly been keeping a running tally of what's going on around the ranch. It's been one horrible day after another, and I've been keeping close to my family. Sue me if I've failed to keep track of every cowboy that's been hired in that time."

"In that time?" Nick repeated, shaking his head. He removed his hat and swept a hand through his dark hair before replacing it. "No worries, Princess. Maybe you're just not the type to *actually* notice the help."

"Excuse me?" she said, immediately offended. She hated the way he'd uttered "the help" and how he'd implied that she was snobbish. "I've been a little busy grieving my dad."

A muscle in Nick's jaw twitched. "The stable hands are all aware of your loss, and we're very sorry for that—"

Jillian could hear a *but* coming.

"—but I've been working at this ranch, for your father, living in a cabin a quarter mile down the road for the past *three* years."

Three years? That couldn't be true. Jillian's cheeks heated even as she thought it, redness setting in so quickly she was sure her face was now brighter than the stripe on the Lone Star flag.

"You have my condolences," Nick continued. "Lord knows Archibald was a great employer, and we all had mighty big respect for him around here."

Jillian wondered if that had changed when news of his three separate families made its way around the ranch. They'd tried to keep things quiet, but a secret like that was bound to get out.

"But that excuse doesn't really cut it. It's not like I've been hiding in a bush this whole time."

"I never said you were. Just that we hadn't been introduced." But was he right? Jillian peered at him. Surely she would have noticed a guy like Nick around the stables, working with the horses, before now? He was so dang tall and broad and handsome, how could she have missed him? Or had she just become so blind to the turnover of stable hands at the ranch that she hadn't bothered to notice? She tried to fumble up an excuse, to find some way to explain herself, but the harder she tried, the more she realized there had to be some truth to Nick's words. He looked at her like she was some stuck-up, out-of-touch rich girl, and she was living up to the stereotype. She cringed.

But a second later, irritation flared in her chest, and she knuckled that space between her ribs again. She crossed her arms as pressure built behind her eyes. "Look, all I wanted out of this meeting was to ask you some questions about my dad, not to be accused of... I don't even know what."

Nick cocked his head, his brow arching in a way that fanned her frustration because on top of being annoyed by him, her stomach flipped, a wave of attraction surging through her. She felt betrayed by her own body. Nick could take his rugged cowboy schtick and shove it where the sun didn't shine.

He sighed heavily, surprising her. "You're right."

"Oh, am I?" she snapped. "Are you sure I'm not further offending you?"

A smile cut across his face. "You apparently can't help it."

"Wooooow."

"Dial it back, Princess," Nick said.

She glared at him. "Do *not* call me that." Who was Nick Slater to judge her? Actually, how dare he!

"I dunno… Princess suits you so well. I reckon it must be written somewhere on your birth certificate. Jillian Fortune—crown princess of rare horses."

—and too good to interact with the staff. Was that what he was thinking? She rolled her eyes. "You're ridiculous."

"It *does* say that, doesn't it?"

No wonder they hadn't been introduced these past three years. The universe had probably sensed how insufferable this man was and had tried to spare her the experience. Who cared what Nick Slater thought, anyway? He was just some cowboy. He had no idea who she really was. Because if he did, he certainly wouldn't be calling her a princess.

His words meant nothing, she told herself.

But then why did they sting so badly?

She cleared her throat, doing her best to sound unbothered. "All I want to do is try to help piece my family back together after what happened recently."

Nick's smile thinned. "Mighty tall order, that one."

"I know." In all honesty, Jillian and her dad had never been close, especially after she'd pushed him to spend more time with the family—with *her*—and he'd always come back with some excuse. He'd rarely shown up for her competitions back when she was still show jumping and even after she'd quit and started to follow an acting bug, he'd never found the time to attend any of her school performances. In fact, he'd strongly encouraged her to pursue other extracurriculars, calling acting a "poor use of her time." Maybe those excuses made sense now, knowing he was juggling three families—God forbid she be talented enough to make something of herself and accidentally expose him—but she still didn't forgive him. Yet despite all that, she wasn't heartless.

Their relationship was awkward and complicated and filled with silence more than anything, but she'd still cared about her dad in her own strange way. A rush of emotion filled her, and she choked down a sudden sob.

She would not cry in front of the cowboy. She would *not*! "So…" Jillian lifted her chin, her nostrils flaring as she stared Nick down. "Are you going to help me or not?"

Chapter Three

"Are you going to help me or not?"

Her feistiness surprised him. Nick couldn't say he'd expected it from a girl who probably spent half her week at the salon or brunching with her girlfriends or jetting off to exotic locales to splurge on designer handbags that got buried in a closet never to be seen again.

"Well," she demanded, all but stomping her foot as she tossed her hair over her shoulder. "Are you?"

Nick could tell he'd riled the princess by the slight quiver in her voice. She glared at him defiantly, arms crossed, but behind those hazel eyes—the ones that shimmered like fresh hay under a clear Texas sunrise—she actually looked like she might be about to cry. And now he felt like a real horse's ass. "Look, Ms. Fortune, I didn't mea—"

"Call me Jillian," she interrupted.

"Jillian," he said softly, turning the word over on his tongue. "I didn't mean to upset you."

"You didn't upset me," she replied far too quickly for it to be true.

"*Frustrate* you, then," he amended, his pulse skipping when the corner of her mouth twitched. It wasn't a full smile, but it was something. He really hadn't intended to hurt her feelings; he'd just been surprised that after all this time of him working at the ranch and living nearby, she hadn't once noticed him. Maybe some part of him had even been a little bothered by it… Not that he'd admit that to her.

Because after three years, he sure as hell had noticed Jillian Fortune. Whether it was on those occasions when he spotted her out riding, her long chestnut hair blowing in the breeze, or hurrying out of the main house, dressed to the nines with her sister as they rushed off to attend some function, it was hard *not* to notice her. She was tall and slender and regal looking—the kind of woman that turned heads without even trying. Add in that sweet smile and her soft, lilting voice, and yeah, like so many others, Nick had found himself drawn to that special brand of Fortune charm.

But hearing her admit that she barely knew who he was… Well, it was sort of a punch to the ego. And that was exactly why Nick didn't mix business with pleasure, or go batting out of his league, because people like Jillian lived in a world he could only imagine. And more often than not, they turned out to be huge disappointments. But none of that mattered because he wasn't here to be *noticed* by Jillian. The woman might be a *little miss rich girl*, but she *did* just lose her father, so he needed to do his job.

"I really *am* sorry for your loss," Nick said. He had no desire to rattle her any further or to see just how fiery she could get. He needed this job more than he needed to feel validated, so he softened his attitude. Plus he *was* genuinely sorry. As far as billionaires went, Archibald had always struck him as being very down to earth, at least in the few interactions they'd had.

Jillian nodded briefly. "Thank you."

"I know what it's like to lose a close family member," he continued. "I'd like to say it gets easier but… Well, I think the pain fades eventually, but the remembering is always hard."

Jillian's eyes narrowed slightly, her head tipping to the side like he'd said something interesting, and as he took her in, he considered that one wife would be handful enough. He had no idea how Archibald had managed to keep *three* happy. Nick wasn't a gossiper by nature, but after his passing, word around the ranch was that Archibald Fortune's private life was a mess.

He had almost done a double take when he'd first heard about the bigamy. After a month, the shock had mostly faded, but that didn't stop the stable hands from talking. Nick tried to stay out of it, mostly because he still appreciated that Archibald had trusted him enough to have him take care of the land near the railroad tracks—he really needed the extra cash right now. But that didn't stop Desmond Pacheco, fellow stable hand and friend, from filling Nick's head with wild theories about how Archibald had kept multiple families in the dark all these years. They ranged from Archibald having a secret twin to him being in witness protection to him having help from the FBI. Though, at the end of the day, Nick supposed the only person who could really answer the questions of *how* and *why* was gone now. As he looked at Jillian, he considered how frustrating that must be for the wives and children Archibald left behind.

"It's been tough," Jillian admitted quietly, dropping her gaze down to her feet. She almost looked embarrassed. "Dealing with that kind of shock."

"I imagine so," Nick said. She was obviously still unsettled by the news and learning about Archibald's double—*triple?*—life. That would be a lot for anyone to handle, even the child of a billionaire, so he definitely should have cut her some slack. "I know there's nothing else I can say to make it any easier, but I'll help out as best as I can. What were you hoping to get from this meeting?"

Jillian's gaze lifted, her glossy pink lips pursed in thought. He really shouldn't be staring at her mouth, but somehow he couldn't resist. "Do you know why my dad hired you to care for that land?" she asked simply. "I guess I want to start there."

Nick removed his hat, shaking out his hair, and sat down at the end of the oval table. Jillian joined him, pulling out the chair across from him. "Honestly," he replied, "I have no idea why your father hired me specifically."

"You didn't have some sort of connection to him?"

"Besides working at the ranch?" Nick shook his head. "No. When he sought me out to offer me the position, I was surprised myself."

"Can you walk me through that day?" Jillian's eyebrows furrowed, like she was trying to pick apart her father's motivations. Almost as if she might find some clue buried there.

"It was early in the day. I'd just dropped Mandy off at preschool and was filling feed buckets. Archibald was hanging around the stables." He shrugged. "But it wasn't unusual for him to drop by in the mornings, so I said hello and didn't think anything of it."

He remembered Archibald staring out at the pastures, his hands clasped behind his back. He'd been a tall man. Distinguished. Gray haired. Soft-spoken but with a handshake that could crush your fingers.

"On this day, he turned to me and started talking more than normal, asking me how I liked working at Fortune and Daughters Ranch and what my plans for the future might be. We talked about Mandy a bit and how I was happy here.

The role was flexible and allowed me to provide for her, making sure she was safe and cared for."

"And then he just said he had some land for you to look after?" Jillian asked.

"Sort of." Nick replayed that day in his mind. It was actually the last time he'd spoken to Archibald before his heart attack. "He said he was impressed with my work ethic and that he'd been keeping an eye on the way I cared for his prized horses and how I'd looked out for Mandy since she was orphaned."

A muscle in Jillian's jaw tensed. She looked *upset* as she glanced down the table to where Mandy sat. Nick wondered if it was lost on her that her father, as busy as he was with his airline and secret families, had managed to notice all those things about some lowly ranch worker.

"Anyway," he continued, "he showed me a picture of this underdeveloped, overgrown land on his phone. He said it was on the other side of town, out past the railroad tracks, and that if I was interested, he was looking for a caretaker."

"So you accepted?" Jillian prompted.

He nodded. "First I asked him a little more about the land. How much there was and what exactly he wanted done with it."

"What did he say?"

"Only that it meant a lot to him. And that he wanted it checked every couple of weeks. The perimeter, the fencing—"

"And if there was a problem?" Jillian interrupted. "Who were you supposed to tell? Him?"

Nick shook his head. "No, he said I was to bring it up with his attorney."

She sighed, drumming her fingers against the table.

"That didn't seem strange to you?" she asked, biting her bottom lip in a way that drew Nick's eye again.

"A little, I guess. But he said I could work the job around my current schedule with Mandy, and with the extra salary bump… Well, I wasn't about to ask too many questions." His paycheck had gone up by a decent amount, and as a single cowboy suddenly responsible for a small child, that was a big deal.

Jillian frowned. He could tell she was gearing up to grill him some more, but the truth was, he didn't have any more to tell her. It had been a straightforward offer. "Look," he said, his voice a little strained. "After losing my brother and sister-in-law in a car accident last year, I *needed* the money. I wasn't about to look a gift horse in the mouth."

"For Mandy?" Jillian wondered.

"Yes." Nick swallowed hard. "She hasn't spoken much since she lost her parents, and I've been taking her to weekly therapy sessions at Emerald Ridge Memorial Hospital." It was therapy Mandy desperately needed for her selective mutism—an unexpected but important expense. That was partly why he'd accepted the job from Archibald right then and there. He hadn't needed any time to think it over. All he knew was that he'd never had to worry about providing for a child before, but suddenly being an uncle came with a whole heap load more responsibility. And *that* cost money.

"She seemed quite excited to talk princesses," Jillian noted.

"Frankly," Nick said, "I'm a little surprised Mandy spoke to you at all. She's not big on strangers." He sighed. "Probably won't get another word out of her today."

Jillian's expression softened. "I'm sorry for your loss," she said. "And Mandy's."

"Appreciate it," Nick said gruffly. He supposed, in their own ways, they both knew the hardships that came with losing people they loved. That horrible day last year, he'd lost his only sibling, and Mandy went from a happy little girl to barely speaking. "Did you have any more questions about the land?" he asked.

"I guess… Did my dad give you any other details?"

"Like what?" he asked.

"The history, perhaps? How it came to be in his possession? Why he'd held on to it and never developed it?" She tossed her hands up in defeat. "What he intended to do with it?"

"Unfortunately, no," Nick said. "We never got around to talking about it again." These were a lot of questions about some old dirt. This family was clearly full of secrets. He glanced over at his niece. At least he didn't have to worry about that with Mandy. She was very straightforward as far as her life went—princesses and unicorns and oddly shaped chicken nuggets. "Sorry I couldn't be more help."

Jillian slumped back in her chair for a beat. "That's all right. I appreciate you taking the time to talk to me."

Nick wasn't all that sure that was true. He hadn't been able to tell her much more than she already seemed to know. He stood, feeling a little disappointed in himself… Wait, *what*? Why did he care so much about helping Jillian Fortune? According to this woman, she'd barely known who he was thirty minutes ago. He shouldn't feel bad about not being able to provide her with more answers. And yet…he really didn't like her disheartened expression. He fought off a sinking feeling in his gut while Jillian crouched down next to Mandy.

His niece blinked up at her, eyes wide and attentive, before pulling off her headphones.

Jillian's smile oozed warmth. "I just wanted to say that it was very nice to meet you today." She shook Mandy's tiny hand. "It's always good to bump into a fellow princess."

The child gasped in awe, her lips parted in a tiny O, and Nick's image of that stuffy, spoiled, rich girl faltered as Jillian surprised him with her sweet words. Then she climbed to her feet, nodding to Nick, and gave Mandy a little wave as she exited the meeting room.

One thing was certain when it came to Jillian Fortune: the woman was a damn bag of contradictions. Nick stared after her, beating back the sudden desire to know everything about her.

Stay in your lane, he reminded himself. A woman like Jillian was no good for him.

Or for Mandy.

Chapter Four

It was a ten-minute walk from the stables up to the main house. The laneway was bordered on either side by live oaks and desert willows. In a couple months, there'd be large pink flowers adorning the branches. But today they were bare, waiting on the first buds of spring. The house towered at the end of the lane, surrounded by a manicured lawn and neatly trimmed hedges. The cream facade was complemented by a steep, gabled roofline, the rust-red tiles reminding her of the burnt sunsets of summer. As she hurried inside, the arched front entrance welcomed her into the family abode.

"Shelb?" she called as she walked through the front door, having spotted her sister's car out by the garage. "Shelby?"

Her voice echoed through the massive foyer. There was no answer, but Jillian suspected she knew exactly where her sister was.

Shelby was now half staying with her fiancé, Cameron Waite, in his downtown penthouse condo, but when she was home, she could usually be found in the kitchen, sating her growing appetite. Mrs. Pulaski, their white-haired, apple-cheeked personal chef, had been cooking for the family as long as Jillian could remember. Now in her sixties, Mrs.

Pulaski insisted on prepping food for Shelby to take away with her while she was at Cameron's.

Jillian walked down the long hallway toward the back of the house, turning into the kitchen. It was a bright, spacious room with glossy white cabinets, warm wooden fixtures and modern stainless steel appliances. Homey touches like the fresh cut flowers her mother insisted on buying every week from the Emerald Ridge Florist made the space inviting. "Hey," Jillian said, spotting her sister.

Shelby sat on a stool at the massive kitchen island, eating some of Mrs. Pulaski's pierogi with caramelized onion, crumbled bits of bacon and sour cream.

"Omigawd," Shelby said around a mouthful. She held her bowl up, pointing at it with her fork. "Have you tried this?"

Jillian laughed. "Yes. For dinner last night."

Shelby closed her eyes in appreciation then crammed another piece in her mouth, waving her hand in front of her mouth. "So good," she muttered. "So hot." She washed it down with water from her emotional-support Stanley cup.

Jillian glanced at the Tupperware on the counter. "Was that the bowl for you to take back to Cameron's?"

Shelby gave her a wry grin. "Yes. What he doesn't know won't hurt him."

Jillian smirked. She was glad things had worked out so well for Shelby. Cameron doted on her and the baby growing inside of her, and after everything they'd been through this past month with their dad, she was glad Shelby had found that bit of happiness.

"What've you been up to?" Shelby asked, tossing her long, blond hair over her shoulder. It was so different from Jillian's, styled in big, loose curls. At first glance, it would be easy to assume they weren't related, but looking more closely, they actually shared the same eyes and nose and prominent cheekbones. Growing up, Jillian had always been envious of Shelby and her perfect princess looks. She used to sit in the crowd at Shelby's beauty pageants and watch her confidently strut across the stage, wondering if she'd look half as good as Shelby if she dyed her hair. Eventually she grew into herself, but she still thought her sister was the prettiest person in every room. And now she had a cute little baby bump to go with it.

Jillian leaned up against the island next to her. "Just finished meeting with the caretaker that's looking after Dad's mysterious land."

"Oh, I forgot that was today!" Shelby said. "I'm forgetting everything. Baby brain! Did you know that was a thing? I swear, it's ridiculous what this little one can do." She pressed her hand to her belly, smiling down at it fondly.

"*Baby brain?*" Jillian teased. "What's been your excuse all these other years?"

Shelby grumbled, trying to prod at Jillian with her fork. "Not funny," she said before stuffing another pierogi in her mouth.

"I'm kidding," Jillian laughed. As the younger sister, it was her job to rile Shelby up. "Just keeping you on your toes. Preparing you for motherhood."

"I'm hoping to make it at least ten to fifteen years before my child starts throwing digs my way."

She grinned. "Oh, I'm going to teach them exactly how to get on your nerves." She was a bit of an expert at it. After all, she'd had a lifetime of practice—borrowing Shelby's clothes without asking, stealing her makeup, peeking in on private text messages with boys.

"Good point. You're only allowed supervised visits with the baby," Shelby joked. "Anyway… How'd it go? What'd you find out?"

Jillian sighed, pulling out one of the stools, and sat down.

Her sister winced. "That bad, huh?"

"No, I mean..." She didn't exactly know how to put into words her encounter with Nick Slater. What did she talk about first? How handsome the man was? How judgmental? How he hadn't been able to tell her much of anything about the land? Jillian started with the thing that bothered her most. "Have you ever noticed a cowboy on the ranch—tall, dark hair, early thirties?"

Shelby laughed at the description. "You'll have to be more specific than that. Next you'll be telling me he wears a Stetson and blue jeans."

Jillian rolled her eyes. Okay, maybe that *was* a bit generic. "He's got a little girl with him."

"Oh, yes," Shelby said immediately. "That's Nick and Mandy. I was so sad to hear what happened to her parents. Poor little thing barely utters a word now. Nick really stepped up to take care of her this past year." She stroked her belly, looking thoughtful. "Why do you ask?"

"Because Nick's the new caretaker of Dad's parcel of land," Jillian muttered. The fact that Shelby knew *exactly* who she was talking about stung, hitting her right in that place between her ribs again. It had taken her sister all of two seconds... Did that mean Nick was right in calling her a princess who couldn't bother to learn the names of the people who worked for her dad? Who kept the ranch running? *Was* she a snob? Unease filled her to the brim. Jillian felt like she was about to overflow with the uncomfortable feeling. He must be right or else it wouldn't bother her so much.

"What's wrong?" Shelby asked, nudging her arm gently.

"Nothing," Jillian was quick to say. She was almost mortified by the exchange with Nick now.

"Jilly, I *know* that face," Shelby said. "You get all scowly and these lines pop up between your eyebrows when something's wrong."

Jillian rubbed at her forehead. "I do *not* get lines!"

"You do. You also pout a little, your lips pursed just like they are now."

Jillian pulled her bottom lip between her teeth. Shelby could read her easier than a book.

She laid her hand on Jillian's where it pressed flat against the island. "What's bothering you?"

Jillian turned her head a fraction to look her sister in the eyes. "Do you think I'm a snob?"

Shelby burst into an unexpected fit of giggles. "Is that a serious question?"

"Yes," Jillian insisted, pulling her hand free to gesture dramatically. "I wouldn't have asked if it wasn't! Now answer honestly."

"*Why* are you asking that?" Shelby wondered, her eyes narrowing slightly.

"Because of…" She sucked in a breath and released it. "Something Nick said while we were talking. 'Maybe you're just not the type to *actually* notice the help.'"

"Why would he say that?"

"Because I didn't know who he was," Jillian muttered awkwardly. "Because he's been working here and living nearby for three years, and I wouldn't have known him from Adam," she continued, "but you seemed to recognize him right away. And you've obviously talked to him enough to know all about Mandy and her struggles."

"Only in passing," Shelby said. "It's not like we're having long conversations out on the porch."

"But still!" she moaned, laying her head down against

the cool marble countertop. “I *am* a snob. I’m a horrible ‘little miss rich girl’ cliché.”

Shelby pushed her plate of pierogies away. “Well, maybe a little.”

Jillian shot up like a rocket. “You’re supposed to make me feel better.”

Her sister shrugged. “I’m sure we’re all snobby in our own ways. You, me, Mama. It’s probably something we could all do with working on.”

Jillian pouted. This conversation wasn’t making her feel any less rotten about herself.

“But…” Shelby continued.

“Argh! I don’t know if I want to hear this *but*.”

“Do snobs volunteer to read to children recovering from surgery in the hospital?” she said pointedly. “Do they visit kids who are stuck in the wards over the holidays, entertaining them with little plays and performances? Do they provide regular deliveries of toys and games for the hospital’s activity room? I don’t think so.”

Shelby needled her in the side until Jillian smiled a bit.

That made her feel slightly better, but a lingering thread of guilt ate away at her. She needed to work on being a better person, especially being more present with the people in her life. Shelby was just so open and extroverted. It was the reason she’d thrived in the pageant scene her whole life. And as much as she’d always wanted to be just like her older sister, Jillian’s time on a stage had come and gone.

When Archibald had reacted so poorly to her acting pursuits, Jillian had set those aspirations aside, coiling in on herself a little more. Maybe her dad was right, and it would have been a waste of her time. Maybe she would have been terrible, only embarrassing herself and the family. But sometimes she put on silly voices with the kids at the hospital or created fun characters to go with her little performances, and she'd remember how much she'd loved it.

"What are you doing during your volunteer shift today?" Shelby went on. "Rocking newborns or something?"

Jillian nodded. Only the ones whose parents or caregivers were unable to take time off work to see them. "But even that's only because I can do whatever I want, *anytime* I want," Jillian said. "I don't have to worry about showing up on time for some nine-to-five or supporting a family. If I want to sit in the nursery all day and rock babies, I can."

"Don't do that to yourself," Shelby said. "Sure, we're well off. And yes, we are super privileged and fortunate for that. Money gives us freedoms other people don't have. But that money can't buy happiness or save us from losing the people we love. So, yeah, maybe you were a bit of a snob today with Nick. But you're also trying to help the rest of us figure out this mess Daddy left behind."

Jillian swallowed hard. *Yeah, thanks for the mess, Dad.*

"I think you can cut yourself some slack. You're entitled to withdraw and process your feelings like the rest of us."

She nodded at Shelby's words. Sure, that was her excuse for the past month. But that didn't explain away the last three years that she hadn't bothered to notice Nick or, frankly, any of the other staff that worked the ranch. The only staff Jillian really bothered with were Mrs. Pulaski, because it felt like the woman had been around since the dawn of time, and Roxie, their housekeeper, who'd once taught Jillian how to do the perfect winged eyeliner. In many ways, Mrs. Pulaski and Roxie felt more like family. They weren't—

Ughhh! She rubbed at her eyes. She really was a snob! She needed to be a *better* person. Her thoughts drifted to their dad, wondering for the millionth time why he'd needed three wives? Three families?

"Did Nick say anything else?" Shelby wondered.

"Aside from repeatedly calling me a princess?" Jillian muttered, which got a little smile out of Shelby. "Not really."

"By any chance did you happen to notice how handsome the man is?"

Jillian scoffed. "I was a little busy being insulted."

"Mm-hmm," Shelby hummed, her lips twisting in amusement.

"Anyway," she said, getting back on track before her sister got any ridiculous ideas. "I guess Dad saw the way Nick cared for the horses and Mandy and decided he would take good care of the property. Nick's supposed to keep it neat, make sure the fencing is in good condition…that kind of stuff. If there are any issues, he's supposed to take it up with the attorney. Other than that, he has no information on the land."

"Hmm." Shelby climbed off her stool to look in the fridge. "Guess that's a dead end then. Hopefully we'll have more luck with Lianna Dunhill's aunt this week."

Talking to the aunt of her dad's deceased mistress was next on their list to tackle, though after today's disappointment, Jillian wasn't confident it would bring them any closer to discovering the identity of this missing heir. She supposed they had to try though.

"You want some dessert?" Shelby asked.

"No, I'm not hungry."

Her sister reappeared with a bowl of berries and a can of whipped cream, looking elated. "Don't roll your eyes at me."

"I didn't roll anything," Jillian said, smirking.

"Mama and I are going shopping," she continued. "I need to fuel up."

"Shopping for baby things or wedding things?" Jillian asked

Shelby shrugged. "Probably both. You want to meet us after your volunteer shift?"

"Can't. I'm getting coffee with Melissa and Rory to talk about how horrible cowboys are."

Shelby smirked. "I think you mean horribly handsome."

Jillian *did* roll her eyes then. So hard it hurt.

"Speaking of hot men," Shelby said. "How is your love life these days? I feel like I'm missing out spending half my time at Cameron's."

"Virtually nonexistent," Jillian admitted, though truthfully she hadn't thought much about dating in the month since losing Dad.

"What about the last guy?" Shelby said. "Brian… No, Brendan?"

"*Brandon*," Jillian corrected.

"Yes, him. I thought you two were having fun?"

"We were," Jillian said, shrugging. "But it didn't go any further than fun. I feel like the guys I'm dating…" Mostly the trust-fund guys. "Well, I *do* have things in common with them, which is a start. But no real chemistry." Honestly, she'd had more chemistry with Nick, despite the fact they'd been getting on each other's nerves for half the conversation.

"Well, chemistry is important," Shelby agreed. "If you're just not feeling it, no use in dragging it out, I suppose."

"Exactly. There's no real promise to any of the relationships," Jillian explained. "Recently it feels like all the guys are hesitant to commit, and that reminds me a little too much of Dad."

"Aww, Jilly, don't do that."

Jillian shrugged. Money made it easy to flit from one woman to the next—her dad had proven that by having three wives and a mistress—and that was the last thing she wanted. What she wanted was something *real*, something with a little passion. She was looking for the kind of spark she'd felt during that brief meeting with Nick.

For some reason, that idea sent her mind spinning to thoughts of marriage and children. Maybe it was because she'd watched him sweetly dote on Mandy or because she was spending too much time with her pregnant sister. Either way, she'd never once been interested in those things before, happy with her whirlwind "princess" life. But now she was envisioning a white-washed porch and babies crawling across hand-knitted blankets and *Nick* wearing his damn, dusty blue jeans.

She glared at Shelby.

"What?" her sister tipped the whip cream can straight into her mouth.

"You're making me all emotional thinking of marriage and babies. About *wanting* that one day," Jillian said. "Ew, you're rubbing off on me. Keep those hormones to yourself!"

"This has nothing to do with my hormones," Shelby said, laughing. "And there's nothing wrong with wanting that. Maybe you had a little bit of a spark with Nick."

"I don't know that I'd call it a spark."

"But you *did* think he was attractive," Shelby reminded her. "Even with him calling you a snob."

"He didn't call me a snob, he insinuated it." Jillian crossed her arms. "And anyone would think he was attractive."

"But did *you*?"

"By society's standards, I suppose he is aesthetically pleasing."

Shelby smirked. "It's not a bad thing, you know, having a little spark. You deserve some happiness in the midst of all the craziness we're dealing with. And maybe it's time to take a break from the trust-fund guys."

A break with Nick? No way!

"Seriously," Shelby said, sounding a little too excited. "Whatever you felt could turn into a *great* thing."

"I mainly felt annoyance," Jillian said, denying her attraction. "And there is no *thing*."

"Well, not with that attitude," her sister huffed.

Jillian shook her head, fighting off an amused smile. "I've gotta run for my hospital shift. See you when I see you."

Shelby nodded. "I'll be here. Mama and I can do a baby haul to show you what we got."

"Sounds good." Jillian grabbed her car keys and headed for the door, determined to put thoughts of Nick Slater from her mind, though part of her couldn't stop thinking about what Shelby had said. *Whatever you felt could turn into a* great *thing.*

Jillian didn't know if she was ready for that right now. But was her sister right? Did she need something a little different as far as her love life was concerned? Or just life in general? Being directionless was getting kind of old, and the truth was, she wanted a taste of the happiness that Shelby had found.

She wanted to find her purpose.

Chapter Five

"All right, Squeaks," Nick said as he pulled into a parking spot in the garage outside the Emerald Ridge Memorial Hospital. He turned off his truck then turned around, facing Mandy. "We're gonna do some good work today, right?"

She nodded once, holding an assortment of toys in her lap. Nick swore more of them appeared every day. He was always pulling out stuffies and books and crayons and costume jewelry and all sorts of other little girly things from between his seats. He didn't know where the toys kept coming from. All he knew was that they seemed to multiply dangerously, and he feared that one day he'd open the door to find a tidal wave of them spilling out onto his feet.

"You're gonna go in there and talk Trisha's ear off, okay? Tell her all your news. Everything you did this week."

Mandy nodded again.

Nick smiled softly, letting out a heavy breath. She was probably lying right to his face, but she didn't know any better. And Trisha, her counselor, always told Nick to make the sessions sound exciting. To make them into something Mandy *wanted* to attend.

"All right," he said. "Good talk."

He opened his door and climbed out, walking around the end of the truck to open Mandy's door. She looked at him expectantly as he unbuckled her from her car seat. Once she was free, the toys toppled off her lap and onto the floor. Nick shook his head.

"We've gotta get you a bucket or something to keep these things corralled."

Mandy climbed down from the truck, knocking toys out as she did. Nick scrambled after them, tossing things back through the door while making a mental reminder to clean his truck up later. Between her toys and Otto's—the emotional support labradoodle he'd adopted to help Mandy come out of her shell—his truck was quickly turning into toyland.

"Hand," he said, thrusting his arm out in Mandy's direction. He'd learned very quickly that small children had a penchant for running off in parking lots. It was like some strange biological urge. Nick didn't know when humans developed a sense of self-preservation, but it clearly wasn't at four. He wriggled his fingers at her, and she finally latched on to his hand, hers so tiny he sometimes felt like he had to protect her from the entire world.

"Okay," he said, narrating their next steps. Trisha had suggested it to him early on in the counseling sessions. Mandy didn't often respond or initiate conversation, so it was easy to forget that she actually *needed* to be part of the conversation. It had taken him a while, but Nick had gotten used to keeping up a one-sided stream of chatter. "We get the parking ticket and then where do we put that?"

Mandy pointed back to the truck.

"Right. We put it on the dashboard so security doesn't give Uncle Nick a ticket."

Mandy gave him a little thumbs-up.

"Then we'll head inside to see Trisha and tell her all about your visit to the stables this morning."

He led his niece to the corner of the garage, where a payment machine beeped. Honestly, Nick thought, the person who'd decided to charge parking fees to take children to the hospital should be jailed.

"Bring any quarters?" he asked, looking down at Mandy.

She wrinkled her nose, her eyes narrowed with amusement, and pointed at him.

"*My* job?" Nick said. "Excuse me, little lady. Why's it always my job to bring the money?"

She shrugged.

"Why do I suspect you'll still be saying that when you're fourteen and asking for money to go to the mall?"

Mandy pointed at the blinking green light.

"Hold your horses," Nick mumbled, digging around in his pockets for enough change to feed the machine. He could have just used his credit card, but Mandy liked to slide the coins into the slot, and he couldn't deny her when she looked up at him with such glee. So he hoisted her up onto his hip and gave her a handful of change.

The preschooler dropped the coins into the machine, one at a time, really, *really* s-l-o-w-l-y. "Got it down to a fine science there, Squeaks."

Mandy's little face was screwed up in concentration, her tongue caught between her teeth. Nick huffed a laugh. This was why they left fifteen minutes early.

When she finished her weekly chore of paying for parking, the machine spit out a ticket. Mandy snatched it, holding it up triumphantly.

"Winner, winner," he declared, bouncing her in his arms. Sometimes he got her to respond with "chicken dinner," but today was not one of those days. They returned to the truck, tossed the ticket onto the dashboard and headed inside.

The hospital lobby was bustling this afternoon, people

coming and going from appointments while doctors and nurses and other medical staff made their ways to and from work. Nick's nose twitched. The place smelled vaguely of antiseptic, and he shook off the memories that always surfaced of his brother and sister-in-law. That day in the hospital—the day he'd lost them—had been the worst day of his life. And even though the sight of any doctor now made his skin crawl, he marched through these doors every week because it was what his niece needed from him.

They went straight for the elevator, where Mandy pressed the button for the fifth floor, and exited into a long hallway that led to the children's department. Nick released her hand, and she skipped along beside him, following a set of pawprint stickers that had been placed on the floor, creating a fun trail for kids to follow.

"You think we're gonna find the cat that made those today?" Nick said. He asked her that same question every week.

"No," she said, looking at him funny. And well, hey, that was the most words he'd gotten out of her since this morning. Though he supposed she'd used up more than her usual daily allotment with Jillian. Nick's thoughts briefly returned to the woman. As far as meetings with his deceased boss's daughter went, things probably could have gone better. He sort of regretted getting so bent out of shape. Why the hell would Jillian Fortune care about who he was or what he was up to? They lived totally different lives and ran in separate social circles. That had never been more clear than it had been today. Though she'd been extra sweet with Mandy, clearly very comfortable with children, and her kindness had sort of confused his initial impression of her. He wasn't quite sure how to feel about that. But there was actually no need to feel *anything* because he had more important things to focus on right now.

The cat pawprints on the floor turned to horse hooves, and Mandy trotted along, holding pretend reins. "What do you think made those?" Nick asked.

She drummed her lips together, making a buzzing sound. It was her imitation of a horse, and it wasn't half bad.

"Definitely a horse, I'd say."

They turned a corner, passing a bank of offices, then reached a round circulation desk, where Nick checked in for Mandy's appointment with one of the medical secretaries. The space was decorated with bright, cheerful colors. Hand-drawn pictures filled the wall behind the desk. And all the doctors and nurses wore scrubs with funky patterns and usually handed out stickers.

Nick passed over Mandy's health card while she ran off to the dedicated playroom. It was designed in a jungle theme, with a large mural of a cascading waterfall and monkeys swinging on vines. There were several shelves stacked with toys and books and games, and a central table where kids were gathered, some wearing hospital gowns and others likely waiting around for appointments like Mandy.

The fact that she ran around the room so unbothered was a major improvement compared to when Nick had first started bringing her here for her therapy appointments—a mix of speech-language and child psychology. Back then it was nothing but tears and hiccupping sobs and her tiny fingers latched on to his shirt.

"Here you are," the secretary said, handing Nick back the card.

"Thanks." He slid it into his wallet then walked over to lean against the doorway of the playroom, watching his niece. He always let her be when they were here, hoping if he did, she might make herself a friend, but no luck so far. She stopped to peruse one of the bookshelves as they waited for Trisha. They'd been seeing her for months now. When Mandy had first stopped talking after the accident, he'd taken her straight to the doctor and gotten the diagnosis. It had scared him at first. He had no idea how to help a child with selective mutism, but then they'd been linked up with several free counseling sessions, and Nick found that it had been as beneficial to him as it was to Mandy.

Though those few sessions hadn't been nearly enough, so Nick had started paying out of pocket for weekly visits, hoping to get Mandy to talk through her loss. She'd opened up somewhat over the past year, but she still hardly said more than a few sentences a day if he was really lucky. And now that she was in school, the other kids were starting to notice how little she spoke, which had him more worried than ever.

Sometimes when Nick picked Mandy up from the classroom, the other kids would giggle and ask him why she didn't talk. If she didn't start communicating with them, he knew she'd have a harder time making friends, and Nick hated to think about her being bullied. Adopting Otto had been a last ditch effort to speed things along, and though the little girl had taken to him like a fish to water, she hadn't become any more vocal, and the labradoodle now spent most of his time slobbering on Nick's couch.

Trisha had assured Nick that this sort of thing just took time. That Mandy would start speaking when she was ready. But what if she *never* did? What if she always struggled?

"Hi there, Mandy," Trisha said, wearing a giant smile as she walked through another door into the playroom. "And Uncle Nick."

Nick lifted his hand in a hello.

The counselor crouched down in front of Mandy. "What do you say we go play, huh?"

Mandy dutifully ran over and snagged Trisha's hand.

The woman caught Nick's eye. "See you in thirty?"

Nodding, he made his way out to the tiny waiting area in the hall. He slumped down into one of the hardback chairs, trying to get comfy. Sometimes he had company out here, but today it was quiet, and Nick sent off a text to his mother with a picture of Mandy attached. He liked to update her a couple times a week. Losing his brother had been hard on all of them. Nick made a mental note to take his niece out to see her in the near future. He just had to find some time between school and horses and the mysterious land that had the Fortunes requesting meetings with him. Releasing a sigh, he was tucking his phone away just as a tall, gray-haired man in a suit strode down the hall toward him.

"Howdy, Nick."

"Sam," he said, getting to his feet to shake the gentleman's hand. Sam Cartwright was the director of the children's department. He'd been around since Nick had first started bringing Mandy to her counseling appointments and always made an effort to get a smile out of the kid, if not a word or two. Sam reminded him of how far Mandy had come, which Nick appreciated. Sometimes it was easy to lose track of the progress and feel discouraged.

"Mandy already inside?" he asked, scanning the playroom.

Nick nodded.

"Good week?"

"She spoke more this morning than she has in a long time," Nick admitted, his thoughts once again flitting to *princess* Jillian.

"Well, hey, that's great news! Sounds like she's making some real progress during her visits." Sam clapped Nick on the shoulder. "I'm on my way to a meeting, but tell her I say hello?"

Nick nodded. "Will do."

He sat back down. He hoped the man was right and that this progress continued. The thought of hearing Mandy yak in her car seat while they drove through town seemed like such a strange concept, but he couldn't help but smile. She *had* come a long way, and Nick was prepared to do whatever it took to help her get to that point. Mandy was his focus. She had been since the moment he got that horrible phone call about his brother.

It was crazy how life could shift so suddenly. In one single moment, he'd become responsible for a *child*. He wasn't gonna lie, that in itself had been a hard transition. When it happened, his ex-girlfriend, Sylvia, had sat him down and told him she couldn't stay. She'd had no interest in Saturday zoo trips or in sharing her boyfriend with a child. He'd managed to put those feelings to bed now, *mostly*, but when she'd first had the conversation with him, it had been difficult to hear. At the time when he'd needed her support, the person he thought cared about him most in the world had completely bailed.

For some ridiculous reason, Nick tried to envision fancy-pants Jillian Fortune at the zoo on a Saturday, her long brown hair blowing in the breeze, her hazel eyes crinkled at the corners as she—

He shoved that thought from his mind as quickly as it appeared. Despite how gorgeous she was and how taken Mandy was with her, he wasn't interested in entertaining any kind of attraction right now. So these feelings he had, whatever they were, could just take a hike. He'd already learned this lesson with Sylvia—feelings meant caring, and lowering your defenses only opened you up to loss. And he'd lost enough recently. He thought of his brother and sister-in-law, about all the time they were going to miss with Mandy now, and he resolved to be the best uncle he could be in their absence.

Thirty minutes passed quickly, and the next thing Nick knew, Mandy was running down the hall in his direction, smiling. She had a sticker of a happy face stuck to her shirt. Nick got to his feet, and the child threw herself at him like she always did after a session, wrapping herself around his legs. She looked up at him and grinned.

"Did you have fun with Trisha?"

Mandy nodded.

"What did you do?" Nick asked. He already knew what they did, but Trisha had encouraged Nick to ask her questions, even when he knew she wasn't going to answer.

"Played," Mandy whispered into his leg.

"We sure did play," the counselor said, coming down the hall. "And we drew some princess castles."

"Those good old princesses," Nick deadpanned. "They're making the rounds apparently."

"Same time next week?" Trisha asked.

Nick nodded. "We'll see you then." He nudged Mandy. "You gonna say bye?"

Mandy lifted her hand, waving.

With the appointment finished, Nick took the little girl's hand, and they set off down the hall. But before they exited the children's department, a familiar face showed up.

"Hey, y'all. There's my favorite visitors!"

Mandy squeezed Nick's hand in excitement.

Andrew Warner was a pediatric nurse, father of three and one of Nick's very best friends. He was funny, great with kids and had been a huge source of support as Nick got used to the responsibility of a child. Andrew often snuck off during his breaks to catch up with Nick and check in on Mandy's progress when they were here for appointments. "How's it going today?"

"About the same," Nick said, patting Mandy's head. "No tears, though."

"No tears?" Andrew said, getting down on one knee. "Well, that's amazing! You had a good time?"

Mandy nodded shyly. And then, like she usually did, she pointed to Andrew's pocket, silently demanding payment.

Andrew produced two stickers. "Okay, here are today's options. A sparkly unicorn or a farting dinosaur."

Mandy pointed at the unicorn.

"You sure you don't want the dinosaur? I hear their toots smell like rainbows."

Mandy giggled and shook her head, taking her unicorn sticker.

"Catch up soon?" Andrew asked, glancing up at Nick. "Courtney's away this weekend, so I'm in full dad-mode. I'm thinking a park and pizza kind of day."

Mandy gasped in excitement.

"What d'you think, Squeaks?" Nick looked down at Mandy. "Park and pizza?"

She threw her hands up in excitement.

Andrew grinned. "I'll take that as a yes."

Chapter Six

Jillian was never late for her volunteer shifts. Years of early morning riding sessions and a strict boarding school had developed a strong sense of punctuality in her.

But she'd obviously spent too much time complaining to Shelby about Nick Slater.

Nick Slater!

She really needed to stop thinking about him. That was what she'd taken away from their meeting this morning. That and the realization that tracking down her dad's mysterious, maybe nonexistent heir was going to be a lot more challenging than she'd assumed. If she couldn't even figure out why her dad had held on to *that* particular piece of land or why it had been important enough to him to hire a caretaker, then how were they supposed to find out anything about their missing sibling? No heir, no inheritance. No inheritance, no horses.

Jillian had weathered enough change recently. She wasn't ready to say goodbye to King too.

She shoved those thoughts from her mind, digging her volunteer badge from her purse and pinning it to her shirt as she hurried through the hospital lobby. She lifted her hand, waving to Patrice at the patient help desk. When she'd first begun volunteering, she'd started there, eventually making her way over to the children's department, where she felt like she made the most difference.

Behind the help desk was the now-empty gift shop. It had sold mediocre coffee and greeting cards until a bad leak had shut them down. The gift shop had been relocated closer to the cafeteria while repairs took place and had never returned. Now the space sat empty. Stifling a yawn, Jillian knew she sure could use a cup of coffee right about now. But the hospital cafeteria was too far out of the way. If she made the detour, she'd definitely be late, and that meant less time cuddling with adorably tiny babies.

So she put her need for caffeine to the back of her mind and made her way over to the elevator, pushing the call button. People gathered around her, waiting as well, some of them probably patients destined for an appointment, others health care workers on their way back from break. Resisting the urge to impatiently tap her foot, she pulled out her phone to check the time. She'd probably only be a couple minutes late, which wasn't horrible, though she usually liked to have some time before her shifts to catch up with the nurses. It was better than any episode of *Real Housewives*, and right now Jillian could use the distraction.

The elevator doors opened, and she looked up from her phone as the crowd surged forward. She froze in place as Nick and Mandy flooded out. He had the girl on his hip, keeping her from being crushed in the back and forth of people.

"Jillian!" Mandy said, pointing right at her.

Nick blinked at his niece, his eyebrows arched with surprise. "That's right."

"Hello again," Jillian murmured, smiling at her.

They stepped out of the path of people. As Nick set her

down, Mandy thrust her arm out, showing off a sparkly sticker.

"What've you got there?" Jillian asked, leaning down to see. "Oh, a unicorn!"

Mandy nodded, smiling.

"That's an excellent choice in steed for a princess."

The child's eyes lit up and she leaned against Nick's leg, looking very pleased with herself.

"What are you doing here?" Nick asked as she lifted her gaze to look at him. It wasn't awkward, exactly, she just hadn't expected to see him so soon after their meeting. So much for *not* thinking about Nick.

"I'm not stalking you," Jillian said. "If that's what you're worried about."

Nick huffed a laugh. "I didn't think you were. No one wants to spend their free time at the hospital." His eyes flickered down to the badge on her shirt. "Unless..."

"I volunteer here," she told him. "Usually in the children's department."

"Oh," he said, looking even more surprised than when Mandy had called her name. "We've never bumped into you before..."

"I'm in the NICU most of the time," she explained. It was on a different floor than the rest of the youth services. "Rocking newborns."

"Really...wow?"

"Well you don't need to sound *that* surprised," she said. "I am capable of things other than snobbery."

"I meant *wow* as in I didn't realize that was a job," he clarified. "I never called you a snob."

He hadn't. He'd merely insinuated it this morning. A small part of her hoped that she'd proven him wrong. At least a little. Maybe she wasn't perfect, but she did have a heart and a desire to do better, to *be* better. To use her privilege in a way that helped her community. Though she couldn't even attempt to do that without her portion of the inheritance. "That's true," Jillian said. "I think you drew the line at *princess*."

"Which is valid." He gave her a crooked smile. "For multiple reasons."

Jillian crossed her arms, yet a smile tugged at her mouth. "Well, just so we're clear, I might live this princess lifestyle, but I'm not a horrible person."

"I never thought you were horrible."

"Good," she said.

"Great."

"Cheeseburgers!" Mandy said excitedly, interrupting them.

Jillian blinked down at her. So did Nick.

"What was that?" Jillian asked.

"Cheeseburgers?" Mandy said again.

Jillian looked to Nick to explain, but he already seemed to be scrambling for something to say. "Uh, I think… Well, we're having cheeseburgers for dinner tonight."

"Before or after the ice cream you promised?" Jillian asked.

Mandy gasped, looking at him like she'd just remembered. She tugged on his pant leg.

"Thanks for that," Nick muttered.

Jillian smirked. "Happy to help."

"Come?" Mandy said to Jillian, giving her a shy smile before hiding her face in the side of Nick's leg.

"Oh," Jillian replied, somewhat awkwardly. "That's a very lovely invitation, sweetheart."

Nick visibly paled before her. *Oof*, Jillian thought. If the idea of her showing up for dinner was that horrible—

"She's probably very busy, Mandy," Nick said, placing his hand on the back of her head. "She doesn't have time to come for dinner tonight."

Jillian frowned. What did he know about how busy she was? It wasn't like she had dinner plans at Cucina every night. Sure, she enjoyed the occasional meal out with friends, but she usually ate at home. And with her mother off running wedding errands or making preparations for her first grandchild, and Shelby spending a lot of her time with Cameron, more often than not lately, Jillian found herself eating by herself. She hadn't actually realized just how lonely that had become until this very moment.

"And I'm sure Jillian doesn't eat burgers anyway," Nick was saying. Mandy pouted, sticking out her bottom lip.

Oh, boy, Jillian thought. That cuteness was dangerous, and the child had already learned to wield it.

"She's probably vegan or vegetarian or—"

"She is in fact *not* vegan or vegetarian," Jillian said, interrupting Nick. "She actually eats cheeseburgers, if curious minds are wondering, and would *love* to come over for dinner." The words surprised her even as they left her mouth. And they must have surprised Nick, too, because his jaw dropped.

"You're serious?" he mumbled, looking perplexed. Mandy danced excitedly by his side.

"Unless you plan on rescinding my invitation," she challenged. "Which would be considered the height of rudeness."

"No, of course not," Nick said before offering her an uncertain, dimpled smile. There was something so charming about it that Jillian actually chuckled. "But you really want to come?"

"I really do," she said. She'd agreed, and now she had to

stick to it or else face the wrath of Mandy. "I'll even bring dessert." She looked down at the little girl. "Ice cream with sprinkles?"

Mandy threw her hands up in the air.

"All right, then, princess," Nick said, sounding a little like he doubted she would even show up. "We'll see you tonight. Six o'clock. Don't be late."

Jillian sniffed as he called her princess again, but something in her chest fluttered. "I'm never late," she said.

Well, almost never.

An hour and a half later, Jillian had said goodbye to the most adorable babies, each of them tiny and precious and deserving of all the cuddles. She'd held them against her chest and whispered to them, telling them how frustrating—and gorgeous!—Nick Slater was, even when he was blatantly *assuming* things about her.

"You know what happens when we assume things," she'd told the babies, giving them their first real life lesson. "Everyone looks like an ass."

The newborns hadn't had much to offer in the way of advice, but they sure were cute. Now she made her way to downtown Emerald Ridge to meet the girls at Coffee Connection. Unlike the newborns, Melissa Condor and Cordelia "Rory" Grayson had never once failed Jillian when it came to offering advice. In fact, sometimes they had a little *too much* to say. The two of them gossiped more than a rattlesnake could rattle, but they were loyal and always there to lend an ear.

Jillian parked down the street and walked into the coffee shop, spotting Melissa and Rory on their favorite overstuffed sofa, two large mugs on the table in front of them. They had their heads bent together over Melissa's phone screen, the two of them deep in conversation. Jillian stopped at the counter to order her drink—a chai tea latte—then made her way over, slumping down in the chair across from them with a sigh.

"You look like you've been through the wringer," Melissa said, putting her phone down on the table.

"It's been a long day," Jillian agreed. Or, at least, a day filled with big feelings. And it wasn't anywhere close to being over yet.

"How were the babies?" Rory asked.

"Adorable," Jillian said. "Like always. I just wish I had more arms. So many tiny faces to snuggle." She inclined her head in the direction of her friend's phone. "What were you two looking at?"

Melissa gave her a sly grin. "Trying to find Nick on social media."

Melissa, a bestie from childhood, used to have the nickname Missile for how fast she could take down a shot of tequila. Now she was a part-time fashion influencer, always dressed like she was headed for the runway, and part-time gossip, with a killer sense for business. She spent her days consulting with companies on brand management and could spot a trend from a mile away. Rory, her former college roommate and sorority sister, came to visit Jillian in Emerald Ridge one year and never left. She was the daughter of two environmental lawyers and had a soft spot for animal conservation. When she wasn't on month-long projects volunteering for nonprofits that preserved habitats, she was promoting animal welfare. Rory was the only person Jillian knew who could rock a pair of hip waders as well as she did a pair of Louboutins.

"How's that going for you?" Jillian asked.

"Terribly," Rory admitted. "Tell the man to update his socials."

"We're not on that level yet," Jillian said.

Melissa leaned forward at the same time Rory did. "What level *are* you on, exactly?"

Jillian sat up, shaking her head. "I don't even know, honestly. I can't tell if I like talking to him or hate it. His niece is cute though, so I guess he gets points for that."

"I need more details," Rory said, snatching Melissa's arm. "Something's happening here."

Jillian rolled her eyes. "Nothing is happening."

Melissa and Rory had been inseparable since the moment she'd introduced them, getting along like boots and spurs. They'd bonded over their loud, fun personalities, and now they lived two floors apart in the same condo building. Jillian had no idea what she'd do without the two of them, especially right now, when her life seemed to be changing faster than a summer storm rolled in.

"Wait," Melissa said. "Start with the land first. Any news there?"

"No new leads," Jillian admitted sadly. "Nick didn't have any new information. But Shelby and I still have plans to go visit Lianna Dunhill's aunt this week."

"The mistress," Rory said, waggling her eyebrows. "It's *always* the mistress."

"This isn't a murder mystery," Melissa chided.

"But the mistress's family *always* knows something."

"I sure hope so," Jillian said, seeing as Lianna went and kicked the bucket a good while ago.

"Right, let's circle back to Nick now," Melissa interjected. "Tell us more about this cowboy you can't stop talking about."

"Only because he's *so* annoying," Jillian huffed.

"Mm-hmm," Melissa and Rory said at the same time, their voices practically harmonizing. "We'll just gloss over the whole ruggedly handsome thing, right?"

"He also thinks I'm a snob and a princess."

Rory snorted. "You? The one who falls off a horse face first in the mud and gets right back on?"

"Hey," Melissa said. "Our girl cleans up all right."

Rory snorted. "I'm just saying, anyone who really knows Jillian knows *princess* sort of misses the mark."

"I think it's mostly because he thinks I'm spoiled and stuck-up," she added. "At least, that's the impression I gave him this morning. I might have redeemed myself with the cute babies this afternoon, though."

"Wait, you talked to him again?" Melissa said. "Interesting development. Say more."

"I actually bumped into him at the hospital. He takes his niece there. We got to talking, and she sort of invited me for dinner."

"Dinner!" Melissa cried. "Girl, you went from *grrr, what a jerk* to dinner at his place in what…" She checked her phone. "Like six hours?"

Rory laughed. "Those damn romantic hospitals."

"Why didn't you lead with that?" Melissa demanded.

"Because it's just cheeseburgers," Jillian said. "It's not a clandestine, candlelit dinner. And he didn't even want me there. It was his niece!"

"Cheeseburgers!" Melissa and Rory exclaimed simultaneously, giving each other a look before Rory pretended to swoon into Melissa's shoulder.

"Well, not just cheeseburgers," Jillian amended. "I did promise to get dessert as well."

"I hope that's an innuendo for—"

"Ice cream," Jillian said, heading off Melissa's dirty

thoughts before she could get carried away. "With sprinkles. I promised a four-year-old."

"Boo," Melissa muttered. "That's not the kind of dessert we want."

"Well, it's the kind we're getting," Jillian said. "So you two better just cool it."

Rory hummed thoughtfully. "Maybe I should start talking to some handsome cowboys."

Chapter Seven

"Squeaks, you know anything about lighting the grill?" Nick muttered as he flicked the barbecue lighter again and again. He'd grilled on this thing a thousand times. Why today of all days had it decided not to light?

He twisted his head around, catching Mandy's eye. She stared at him, lips pursed. One eyebrow arched. She looked concerned.

"I don't know why it's not working," he said with a sigh. He dropped his hands to his hips. The grill was on. There was actually gas *in* the tank. He had a plate of burgers at the ready. But no dice. He turned off the grill and closed the lid. "Maybe we'll just give it a minute."

Mandy gave him a single nod from where she sat at her small outdoor play table. Nick had put it out here so she could hang with him while he grilled or did the grounds-keeping or ran Otto around in circles so he'd sleep through the night instead of getting the zoomies at three in the morning. Even now the dog bounded across the yard on the world's longest leash. One day Nick hoped to be able to let him roam, but if he let that dog loose now, he'd end up in the stables in thirty seconds flat, riling up all the horses.

"You want something to drink?" he asked her.

Mandy shook her head.

"Right, what d'you reckon Jillian likes on her burgers?"

His niece tipped her head, tapping her chin in thought.

"The usual ketchup, mustard, relish combo?" Nick asked. "Or d'you think she's more of a goat's cheese, caramelized onions, mushrooms girl?"

Mandy wrinkled her nose at the mention of onions. She was firmly on the ketchup, one slice of cheese and two pickles grind. But to be honest, caramelized onions and mushrooms didn't sound half bad. Maybe he'd toss some of them on the grill too if he ever got the thing working. This was going to be pretty embarrassing if Jillian turned up, right on time, and he had no burgers.

He rubbed his palms on his jeans. Why were they so sweaty?

And why in the world was *he* so nervous?

He wasn't the one who'd invited her to dinner. Mandy had. Though it wasn't like Nick had asked her *not* to come. Maybe part of him still felt a little bad about getting under her skin this morning. Hell, maybe he'd jumped to conclusions. Jillian hadn't struck him as the type to volunteer at the hospital, but clearly there was more to her than he thought. Obviously he needed to stop making assumptions about people because it was making him look like a fool, and he was better than that.

Nick lifted the lid on the grill again. "What d'you think?" he asked Mandy. "Is it gonna work this time?" Her mouth curled into a grin, and she shook her head. "Hey, little miss, you better hope it works, or we're gonna have to make Jillian a grilled cheese."

"Howdy, y'all!"

A car door thumped closed, and Nick looked over his shoulder, abandoning the grill for the moment. Des walked up the driveway, carrying a tray in his hands. He didn't live far, just down the road, in a small cabin similar to Nick's. All the ranch hands usually resided nearby. It made it easier to come and go from the stables over the course of the day for chores.

"Hey," he called back. "What d'you got there?"

Des held the tray aloft. "I come bearing gifts from Mama Pacheco. Brownies, Mandy. Your favorite."

Mandy stood from her table to stare at him through the porch railings.

Aside from his insatiable gossiping about Archibald Fortune's personal life, Des was the definition of a good guy. He helped his mama out on the weekends, went to church on Sundays and was always on the lookout for Mrs. Right. On Friday nights, he used to swing by the cabin to invite Nick to go for drinks with his buddies in town. When Nick had suddenly found himself with a child in tow, Des didn't stop coming by the way a lot of guys might have. Instead, he'd started showing up with beers and baked goods courtesy of his mother, Gloria. She worked in The Clairmont downtown and was always sending over home-cooked meals and sweet treats. Occasionally, she stopped by herself to babysit or to offer Nick some much needed advice. He'd heard that it took a village to raise a child, and he was slowly but surely finding that village.

"These look amazing," Nick said, accepting the tray as Des came up the porch steps. He set it down on Mandy's little table. She stared at it hungrily. "Don't even think about it, Squeaks. You'll ruin your dinner."

She gave him a look that said *if you can get the grill going.*

Nick turned back to Des. "Thank your mom for me."

"Having a party?" Des said, laughing as he eyed up the

stack of burgers set next to the grill. "Or has Mandy's appetite just exploded?"

"Actually, we're having a guest for dinner."

"Oh, a lady friend?" Des asked, needling him with his elbow.

"Not like *that*," Nick said. "Mandy sorta invited Jillian to dinner when we were at her therapy appointment."

"Jillian Fortune?" Des's eyebrows disappeared into his hairline. "You're kidding!" A sly smile curled across his face. "Moving in on the boss's daughter now, huh?"

Ex-boss? *Dead* boss? Nick wasn't sure how to refer to Archibald now that he was gone. "That's definitely not what this is."

"You didn't agree to cook dinner for Ms. Jillian Fortune?" he teased.

"Well, I did. I suppose. Though technically, like I said, I was forced into it by Mandy."

They both turned to her. She blinked up at them.

"Perfecting that innocent eye routine already," Des laughed. "Nice one, kid." He clapped Nick on the shoulder. "Well, I say go for it. Why the hell not? Life's short, man. Might as well enjoy it."

"There's nothing to go for," Nick grumbled. Jillian was the kind of woman he needed to avoid at all costs. Anyone with enough money not to check their bank account daily was someone he'd never have anything in common with. Because he was here pinching pennies and worrying about sending Mandy to college one day, and Jillian was probably buying those heels with the fancy red bottoms. It would be better for everyone if they kept to their versions of reality. But his mother had raised him not to be rude, so he'd have to endure Mandy's dinner guest. It was only one meal after all.

"You never know," Des said. "The two of you might hit it off over a frozen burger patty."

Nick snorted. He really had to get that grill started. "I'll see you tomorrow?"

Des nodded, heading back down the porch steps. "Good luck with wooing your new lady friend."

Nick picked up the lighter again. "Even *friend* is a stretch."

He put the lighter to the grill, clicked it and the flame finally took.

"Well who's this little guy?" Jillian cooed, walking up to the cabin right on time. Nick winced as Otto bounded in her direction, standing up on his hind legs for maximum slobber radius. To her credit, Jillian didn't flinch, instead giving him a good scratch behind the ears.

"Otto, no!" Mandy declared, rushing across the porch to save Jillian from the giant furball.

"What a nice dog," Jillian said to her. "Is he yours?"

Mandy nodded, throwing her arms over the pup. He really *was* just a puppy still, with the boundless energy to prove it, and that was a terrifying thought for Nick to have because he already seemed to be outgrowing the place.

Jillian looked over at Nick. "Something smells good."

"Well, I finally got the grill lit, so hopefully it tastes good too."

"If not, I came prepared," Jillian said, holding up a bag with a tub of ice cream and sprinkles.

"Seems like we've got a feast." Nick looked down at Mandy. "Should we eat?"

She ran back across the porch, throwing the door to the cabin wide open.

"I'll take that as a yes," Jillian said, laughing. Nick liked the sound. He also liked that she was scowling at him far less than she had been this morning. And maybe he even enjoyed the way her hips swayed in those jeans she was wearing. She'd changed from earlier, showing up more casually dressed, and she didn't seem out of place the way he expected she would.

He cocked his head toward the door. "After you."

"What a gentleman," she said.

He nodded. "Mandy has me in training."

Twenty minutes and one meltdown about ketchup later, they were all tucked in at the small, square dining room table. Nick couldn't deny that it was a nice feeling, having the three of them eating together. By the time he'd gotten Mandy moved in and settled after the accident, Sylvia had already moved out, so there hadn't been any dinners for three. Honestly, he sort of liked having another person around to fill the space.

"I thought I was in charge of dessert," Jillian said, nodding to the tray of brownies on the counter.

"Those are from Mrs. Pacheco," Nick explained. "Right, Mandy?"

She nodded.

"Oh, and who is Mrs. Pacheco?" Jillian asked. He liked that she looked directly at Mandy while she spoke, even as Nick answered for her.

"Desmond's mom. He's another one of your stable hands," Nick added for clarification.

Jillian narrowed her eyes at him slightly, but it was more playful than annoyed. He was glad of that. He'd worried that dinner would be awkward, especially with Mandy sitting silently between them, but Jillian filled the space, telling Mandy all about the adventures she used to get up to with her sister on the ranch.

"Did you know we used to have cats all over the barn?" she said to Mandy.

The child's eyes lit up.

"When Shelby and I were little, we snuck a cat into the stables," Jillian went on to say. "We didn't know it at the time, but she was pregnant, and she had her babies in the hay loft. We would climb up to the loft every day to look after them and cuddle with them until they were big enough to venture around by themselves."

Mandy turned to Nick, giving him the *please, please, please* eyes that usually ended with a new toy or tears.

"Oh, no way, Squeaks. You've already got Otto to look after. This place isn't big enough for a dog *and* a cat."

"Otto looks like he could use a friend," Jillian said unhelpfully. She grinned at him, probably knowing exactly what she was doing.

"Otto is a solitary animal," Nick stated. "He prefers it that way."

Jillian bit her lip to hold her laughter at bay. "Sure, Uncle Nick. Whatever you say."

Mandy propped her head on her hand and just stared at Jillian. Nick marveled at her little obsession. For a beat, he wondered if Jillian reminded Mandy of her mother. They hadn't really looked alike, but Theresa had always been sweet and soft-spoken… And she was always smiling. It was that smile that had first charmed Nick's brother, Colton. Nick didn't know what it was about Jillian, but Mandy probably would have happily sat at the table and listened to her recite the alphabet on repeat.

"All finished?" Nick asked his niece once she started pushing pieces of hamburger around her plate.

Mandy nodded.

"I think you did pretty good. Guess that means…"

She pointed to the freezer, where they'd left the ice cream.

"Oh, you can't possibly have room for dessert?" Jillian teased.

"Uh huh!" Mandy nodded enthusiastically.

Nick's heart leapt each time she spoke to Jillian. Each time she used her voice for anything.

"Well, let's round up some bowls." He got to his feet. "Does the princess eat ice cream?"

Jillian settled him with a pointed look. "She does. She even has a favorite flavor."

"Which is?"

"Maybe one day you'll find out." She leaned over and whispered something to Mandy. Presumably her favorite ice cream flavor.

"That's low," Nick grumbled.

"What can I say? Princesses gotta stick together."

"C'mon, Squeaks," Nick said, "give it up. Tell me what she said."

Mandy pretended to lock the words away, twisting her fingers next to her lips.

"Traitor," he said as he doled out ice cream at the counter. Mandy snickered next to Jillian until he put a giant bowl of ice cream down in front of her topped with rainbow sprinkles. Mandy's eyes went so wide both he and Jillian broke into laughter. When they'd finished with their ice cream, the preschooler pointed to the television.

"Only one episode," Nick told her. He was still getting used to the sheer number of kids programs that were available online. Mandy would sit in front of them all day if he'd let her, and he definitely did *not*, worried she'd pull away from the world even more.

As Mandy jumped up to go throw herself down on the

couch with the remote, Nick stood to clear the dishes, and without asking, Jillian offered to help. She probably had people to do this kind of thing for her at home, so he was a little surprised.

"Can I ask you a favor?" Jillian said as she put sticky ice cream bowls into the sink of soapy water.

"What kind of favor?" Nick asked, tossing condiments back in the fridge.

"Can you take me out and show me around my dad's property sometime this week? Other than tomorrow, I can be available whenever you have time between Mandy's schedule and the horses."

Nick nodded slowly. "Of course."

Though he'd agreed, he privately worried about spending even more time with Jillian. He wasn't supposed to find her attractive or sweet or funny. A rich girl like her was bad news with big expectations he could never live up to financially. He needed to stay in his own lane instead of getting himself tangled up in a world he couldn't afford to be a part of. But watching her with Mandy tonight, knowing that she volunteered at the hospital… Well, he knew now that he'd definitely made too harsh a judgement of her earlier. There was a lot more to Jillian Fortune than just her princess persona.

"Hey," he called out to Mandy. "Save the next episode for tomorrow."

She huffed and climbed off the couch, turning off the TV.

"Why don't you go get started on your teeth," he said. "Make sure you actually use toothpaste."

She toddled off down the hall, and a beat later he could hear the buzz of her tiny electric toothbrush.

"Impressive," Jillian said. "Pretty sure getting kids to brush their teeth requires some kind of superpower."

"Oh, we've had many heated conversations about it," he joked. "Usually ends with her stomping her foot at me and marching off in a huff."

"Ah yes, she's joined the sisterhood early," Jillian joked.

Nick rolled his eyes but smiled. "We've gotten better with it recently, though there's every chance she's just in there mucking around in the sink."

They finished cleaning the kitchen, and once Mandy was in bed, Nick found Jillian waiting for him on the couch. Part of him had wondered if she'd take off while he was reading Mandy her bedtime story—one he'd read so many times he could have recited it from memory. He was pleased to find that she'd stuck around, however.

"Can I grab you a drink?" he asked, going to the fridge. "All I have is…beer?"

She laughed. "I drink beer, cowboy."

"Good to know." He retrieved two bottles, popped the lids off and carried them over. Then he sat down on the couch next to her. It was cozy. He forgot what it was like to be around someone like this. Nick batted away thoughts of Sylvia. He didn't need to relive that pain right now. This was *just* dinner—just a friendly meal with someone he wasn't even friends with.

"Is this your brother?" Jillian asked, distracting him from those thoughts. She'd picked up a family portrait off the side table next to the couch. The photo was of him, Colton, Theresa, Mandy and his mother.

Nick nodded. "That's my brother and sister-in-law there with Mandy… She must have only been a few months old. And our mom."

"Did your mom ever consider taking Mandy after the accident?" Jillian asked, looking at him thoughtfully.

Nick shrugged. "She wanted to, of course. But she's not as young as she once was."

Jillian stared at the picture. "She must have had you a little later in life."

"Mid-thirties," Nick said. "Which doesn't seem all that old, until your kids are all grown up with kids of their own," he said. "I make sure to drive Mandy down to visit her as often as I can, but pushing seventy, I know it would be hard to have a four-year-old under foot all the time." He sighed. "And I feel like my mom has sort of done her duty. She raised two boys on her own after losing my dad to cancer. Then she loses my brother and sister-in-law." He shook his head. "Asking her to raise another child felt like too much. And I never wanted Mandy to feel like a burden. I just want to be able to protect her from feeling any more of that heartache."

"My sister said something to me today," Jillian said, sipping her beer before continuing. "She said that all the money in the world can't buy health or protect you from loss. I'd never really thought about it like that. But I suppose life boils down to those same basic things for everyone. So, for what it's worth, I think you're doing a great job with Mandy."

Her words struck him. Again, it occurred to him that perhaps they weren't as different as he'd thought upon talking to her earlier. And he supposed she was right—loving people, no matter who you were, inevitably meant loss, and that was what terrified him so much about opening up again.

"It's definitely been a learning curve," he admitted. "It's not that I never pictured having kids of my own one day…

It's just that I hadn't really considered when that might be. And then, you know, I figured I'd get some practice at it when they were tiny and really just wanted to eat and sleep and poop." He blew out a ragged breath. "But Mandy's already a tiny person with needs and wants and… When I made the decision to take her, I just never assumed I'd have to do this alone. It gave me a lot more respect for my mother, working two jobs to keep us fed and clothed and with a roof over our heads."

"Was there someone around before to help out?" Jillian asked curiously. "If you never assumed—"

"Yeah," he said, awkwardly rubbing at the back of his neck. He didn't know why he felt embarrassed to tell people about Sylvia, about the fact she'd walked out on him. Maybe it was because he felt like he'd failed somewhere along the way. "My last girlfriend bailed when I took Mandy in. So…"

"*What?*" Jillian said, sounding genuinely upset for him. "That's awful."

"It was," Nick agreed. "And really hard to get over. I was grieving the end of that relationship and the loss of my brother, while also trying to care for Mandy. But I've moved past it now." It still hurt his heart, but he understood it better, and with time and distance, he supposed he couldn't fault Sylvia. It had been harsh at the time, but it had been the right decision for her. "She just wanted no part of the 'mom' thing, you know? And I'd never realized that before. She never struck me as someone who wouldn't want kids. But she flat out said she wasn't ready for kids or to be dating a guy that suddenly had a kid, and I guess I respect her for knowing herself enough to not drag either of us through a messy breakup once Mandy had already taken to her."

“That’s very big of you,” Jillian said quietly. “I think I’d still be angry, though.”

“I’m too busy most days to be angry,” Nick told her. Exhaustion hounded him like a cold in the winter. “That’s the one benefit of running around after a kid all day outside of work. You’re too tired to think of much else at the end of the day.”

“But still…” she said. “It’s just hard to build a life with someone and then realize you don’t know them as well as you thought you did. I mean, I’m sure you’ve heard about my dad and his multiple families.”

Nick nodded as politely as he could.

“Well, there you go,” Jillian said, her brow furrowing. “I spent my whole life around the man, and he turned out to be… Well, a liar and a crappy dad a lot of the time. And I’m only now finding out why.”

Nick didn’t have a clue what to say to that. But he did know what it was to lose people. And he also knew what it was to be angry at them. There were weeks and months when he’d hated his brother for leaving him like this to raise Mandy with only a shadow of her parents left behind in old picture frames and photo albums. How was he supposed to make sure his niece grew up knowing how wonderful her parents had been? How did anything in the world make sense now that he’d put his brother in the ground? Actually, now that he thought about it, maybe Nick knew *exactly* what to say. Their worlds had both been flipped upside down. It had happened in different ways, but they both carried a similar hurt in their hearts.

He stared at her, and suddenly she wasn’t Jillian Fortune—heiress, rich girl, princess—anymore. She was just…*Jillian.* Beautiful and sweet and kind. He took her in, her hazel eyes almost gold in the lamplight.

"I guess maybe you dodged a bullet with your ex," Jillian said after a moment. "Maybe something better will come of your life without her in it."

Nick wondered if that was what she kept telling herself about losing her dad. "Do you think any good came from finding out about the other families after all these years?"

Jillian sighed heavily, looking conflicted. "Well, I've got a bunch of new siblings now, which has been..." A small smile grazed her face. "An *interesting* blessing, to say the least. Maybe some of them will turn out to be really great friends in the end. And Shelby's baby will grow up with a bunch of extra aunts and uncles, so that's something."

And this? Nick wanted to ask. The fact that her questions about her dad's land had brought them together in this way. Was that good? The air suddenly felt charged with something he couldn't name, and he swallowed hard in response.

"He's brought a lot of people into my life since he's been gone," Jillian said, leaning toward him a bit. "A lot of unexpected people."

"Some of them pretty charming, I expect," Nick murmured, closing the distance.

She chuckled. "Don't know if I'd go *that* far."

He could feel her breath on his face. It was sweet, like the vanilla ice cream they'd eaten earlier. "You're sure?"

"Pretty sure."

He hesitated a second, giving her time to pull away. But when she didn't, when her eyes dropped to his lips, he tipped toward her, capturing hers in a kiss. Nick's heart hammered against his chest. Was this really happening? He tilted his head, everything tasting of heat and beer and dessert. Desire coursed through him, a feeling he hadn't been aware of for a long time, and his hands yearned to reach for Jillian—to cradle her face, to deepen the kiss—

but she wrenched away before he could, her lip caught between her teeth as her eyes snapped open.

She jumped to her feet. “Thank you so much for dinner.”

Nick blinked at her. *What the hell had he done?*

“Of course,” he replied awkwardly. “Happy to have you. Thanks for indulging Mandy.”

“I’ll see you around,” she said, her voice a bit raspy.

“Soon,” he agreed, climbing off the couch to walk her to the door. “To take you out to the property.”

“Right,” Jillian said, bolting for the door before he could even cross the living room. “Tell Mandy I had a great time.”

“I will,” he promised, and then she was gone. Nick curled his hand around the doorknob, a wave of regret coursing through him. Had he just royally screwed things up?

Chapter Eight

Bisonville, Texas, was exactly what it said on the sign: We'll Charm Your Socks Off.

"Well, that's adorable," Shelby noted, lifting her phone to snap a photo of the welcome sign as they flew past.

Jillian slowed her car almost to a crawl as they approached Main Street, shops and cars and pedestrians crowding in around them. Two towns over from Emerald Ridge, Bisonville seemed to be a quaint little place with charmingly named storefronts. There was a pet supply store called Whiskers's Goods and a bakery called Sugar Blossom Boutique. Down the road, she spotted Lavender Lane, a small candle and fragrance shop, and across the street was The Polka Dot Porch. A rack of colorful children's clothing hung outside on a display.

Shelby gasped as they passed it, taking another photo.

Jillian snorted. "What are you doing?"

"Sending this to Mama. We have to come back here and look for baby things."

"I think three hundred outfits is enough for the first month of your son's life," Jillian quipped. She slowed, letting a group of pedestrians hurry across the street.

Shelby giggled. "This boy's wardrobe is going to be

more extensive than mine. Oh, look!" she said, pointing out The Cozy Cupboard Café.

"Are you hungry again?" Jillian laughed. "We only just ate."

"This baby is never satisfied," Shelby said, rubbing her stomach. "It says they have homemade sourdough bagels!"

"I'm sure Mrs. Pulaski will make you bagels if you ask."

"You can never have too many bagels," her sister reminded her.

"Focus, Shelb," Jillian said. "Lianna Dunhill. We're on a mission, remember?"

Shelby pouted, fluttering her eyelashes at Jillian. How did Cameron put up with this constantly?

"Okay, fine," she huffed. "Let's see what's going on with Lianna Dunhill's aunt, and then after I will take you for bagels."

Shelby beamed. "Excellent. I'm gonna ask for like a pound of cream cheese."

She settled back in her seat as Jillian drove them through the compact Main Street area and out to the edge of town to follow up on the only lead they had on their dad's gold-digging mistress: an aunt by the name of Jeralyn Ward.

"Honestly," Shelby said. "I'm kind of glad Lianna's not around anymore. Confronting her would have been so awkward."

"I'm not," Jillian retorted. Learning that she'd died about ten years ago had been the first complication in their search for their dad's missing heir. "This would all be so much more straightforward if we could just show up at her house and ask her about this supposed child."

"You think she would have welcomed us with open arms and a glass of sweet tea to talk about Daddy?"

Jillian grimaced. "I don't know. I'm just hoping Jeralyn can shed some light on what happened all those years ago."

Shelby's lips twitched, and she released a soft sigh. "It's still hard to think that Daddy… Well, I certainly never would have believed him capable of any of this."

Jillian didn't know what to say. It wasn't like she grew up thinking her dad was a cheating bigamist. But she'd also never thought of him as a saint. She'd wanted more of him in her life, and he'd constantly pushed her away. She could remember sliding the program for her debut stage performance under his office door during her junior year of high school. She'd landed a small part in her school's production of *A Midsummer Night's Dream*. She'd waited all weekend for him to ask her about it. He never had, instead rushing off on business. She'd later found the program crumpled on his desk. Juggling three families had robbed them of so much, but she didn't have any sympathy for him in that regard.

She'd missed him growing up.

And she hated him for that.

Now she hated that they'd been thrust into this situation.

"That looks like the driveway there," Shelby said, pointing out a large stone block that read Bisonville Acres. With the help of an Emerald Ridge resident, a Google search and some additional tips from the private investigator that their new half brother, Hayes, had hired, they'd tracked Jeralyn down to a long-term care facility. It was built on a massive lot surrounded by miles of wooded trail, where people seemed to like to walk their dogs, judging by all the folks milling about with leashes.

"*This* is a nursing home?" Shelby remarked, her eyebrows arching. "It's…"

"Huge," Jillian said, staring out the windshield.

"Gorgeous," Shelby finished, glancing at her sister as they pulled into the parking lot.

The home itself sat on top of a manicured, low-lying hill. The exterior was all polished stone and glass, with neatly trimmed hedges winding up and down pathways along the building's entrance.

"This place looks like it has Michelin-star dining," Shelby mused as they got out of the car and made their way to the front door, where elegant stone columns framed the entrance.

"I'd live here," Jillian said. "You know…when I'm old."

The interior of the building was just as impressive with its high ceilings and tasteful artwork. Soft golden light filled the space, and a calming piano track echoed in the background. Jillian would not be at all surprised to learn that someone was *actually* playing live.

"Hello!"

They turned to the front desk, a massive semicircle of polished wood, where a young woman smiled at them.

"Uh, hi," Jillian said, stepping forward.

"I'm Marie," the woman told them. "How can I help you today?"

"We called last week," Jillian explained. "We were hoping to visit one of your residents today."

"Yes, of course. Who were you looking to visit?"

"Her name is Jeralyn Ward," Shelby said.

The receptionist nodded. "I'll just have you sign in here." She directed them to a tablet on the desk, where they had to input their names and contact information. After that, Marie verified both their IDs. Once she was satisfied, she called a porter to show them through the building.

"Swanky," Shelby muttered out of the corner of her mouth as they followed the young man.

Jillian nodded in agreement.

They came to the end of a hall, where the porter pressed a buzzer next to a large door. A moment later, a nurse appeared. The porter excused himself and hurried off.

"The front desk called and said you were coming," the nurse said, tapping her access badge to the panel next to the door. Her name tag said Katrina. "Jeralyn never gets visitors anymore. What a nice surprise!"

The door buzzed, the metal lock clicking. Jillian exchanged a look with Shelby. She'd spent a lot of time volunteering at the hospital, and she'd never seen anything like this before.

"This is a locked unit," Katrina explained when Jillian asked. "Jeralyn is a resident in our memory care unit. Most of the residents wander, so the door to the unit is locked for their safety."

Ah, Jillian thought. She hadn't spent any time volunteering in a memory unit before. That was good to know, though she had no idea what to expect of the inside of the unit.

They passed through a short hallway and then another door. This one had funny, tinted glass that looked out into a large atrium. Katrina held the door open for them, and it was like stepping into a cartoon neighborhood. Everything was brightly colored and exaggerated to mimic a residential street. The doors of the residents' rooms had been painted like the fronts of houses, with accompanying mailboxes, house numbers and doorbells. In the middle of the large space were several benches and lampposts and even trees in planters. There was a dining room off to one side, a large nursing station and access to a fenced outdoor area. Jillian looked over her shoulder. The door they'd walked through was inconspicuously painted to look like a shelf of library books. That tinted glass seemed to be one-way glass, giving people a view into the unit but maintaining the farce of the neighborhood.

"This is…" Shelby began. "Wow."

"People usually find it quite neat the first time they visit," Katrina said. "Sort of like stepping onto a film set. But I assure you, there is a lot of nursing going on here."

"Does one of these rooms belong to Jeralyn?" Jillian asked.

Katrina nodded. "That blue door there. But you won't usually find her there during the day. She frequents the dining room and the sunroom." Katrina waved them on, leading them across the ward.

There were actual sidewalks painted onto the floor and a stop sign on a door that said EMPLOYEES ONLY. Jillian wondered if these were things the residents might still recognize on a good day.

"How long has Jeralyn been here?" Shelby asked.

"Oh, for some time," Katrina offered. "The dementia's been progressive, getting a lot worse these past couple of years."

They reached a bright, spacious room with various chairs and table setups, the large windows looking out at the tree-lined property.

Katrina pointed Jeralyn out. She was gray haired and smiling at the window, seated in a wingback chair with a cup of tea on a table next to her.

"She's not very lucid," Katrina cautioned. "Not much of a talker, either."

Great, Jillian thought. Another bust.

"There are moments of clarity when we think she recognizes something." The nurse shrugged. "But more often than not, she just enjoys sitting and watching the birds."

"Is it okay to sit with her for a minute?" Jillian asked.

"Of course," Katrina said. "I'm sure she'll appreciate the company."

Jillian and Shelby made their way over and took seats on either side of Jeralyn. Shelby glanced at her, but Jillian lifted her shoulder. She didn't know where to start.

"Hello, Mrs. Ward," Shelby said softly. "My name's Shelby Fortune, and this is my sister, Jillian. It's nice to meet you."

Jeralyn fiddled with the fabric on the arm of her chair, then turned her attention back to the window, staring out at a lawn that was adorned with statues and bird feeders. Birds flitted back and forth, chasing seeds.

"Mrs. Ward," Jillian tried, "we came here to talk to you about your niece, Lianna Dunhill. Do you remember her at all?"

Jeralyn seemed to light up at the name, her eyes widening a bit. "Lianna?"

"Yes!" Shelby said excitedly. "Exactly. Your niece. Can you tell us about her?"

"Lianna," Jeralyn said again, repeating the name over and over like her mind had gotten caught on the word.

Jillian frowned at her sister. This wasn't going well. "Jeralyn," she prompted. "We're trying to find someone."

"Birds," Jeralyn said, raising a thin, shaky finger to the window. "Need seeds."

"I think they're okay," Shelby said sweetly. "They seem to have plenty."

"Seeds." Jeralyn tapped her hand against her knee. "Seeds. Seeds."

Jillian's stomach sank. Perhaps it was only Lianna's name that sparked recognition but nothing else. After a few more minutes of idle chat that resulted in nothing more than the occasional smile from the old woman, they opted to cut their losses.

"It was lovely meeting you, Jeralyn," Shelby told her. Shelby inclined her head, and Jillian followed her out of the sunroom. They made their way back across the unit.

"Some part of her clearly remembers Lianna," Shelby stated.

"But she likely won't be able to tell us anything." Jillian released a frustrated sigh. "Even if we came back another day."

"Have a nice visit?" Katrina asked as they reached the nursing station.

Jillian nodded. "When you said Jeralyn doesn't get visitors anymore," she began, "what did you mean?"

"Oh, well, she used to have a relative that would visit on holidays. That was a long time ago, though," Katrina said.

Jillian eyed Shelby. She wondered if the visits stopped right around the time Lianna supposedly died. If Jillian was a betting woman, she'd guess the mystery visitor was likely her.

"What was she like?" Shelby asked.

"Cagey woman," Katrina admitted, leaning against the desk as she thought back. "Always kept to herself. Then one day she just stopped showing up completely."

Jillian pulled out a photo of Lianna Dunhill, one that had been included in the dossier the attorneys had handed them. The photo was very old and tearing at the edges, but the young woman framed there was beautiful, with dark brown hair and chestnut-colored eyes. The only other thing they knew about her was that she'd lived above a long-gone riverside seafood restaurant called Duff's Catch, where she'd worked as a waitress. "Is this her?" she asked Katrina. "Is this the woman you remember seeing?"

The nurse took the photo and stared at it for a while, then she shrugged. “It's hard to tell. It's been a really long time. The only reason I remember her at all is because the woman always wore big hats and giant sunglasses when she was here. We used to call her ‘the celebrity’ because she was always slipping in and out like she was hiding from the paparazzi.”

“Oh,” Jillian said. That certainly sounded interesting. *What were you hiding from, Lianna?*

“Thank you for your time,” Shelby said. “We really appreciate it.”

Katrina nodded. “I'll walk you out.”

She escorted them back to the locked door then buzzed them through with her ID badge. Shelby bumped Jillian's shoulder as they made their way back to the lobby. “This place is obviously expensive. What do you want to bet Lianna used some of her hush money from Daddy to provide for Jeralyn even after her death?”

“I think that's a safe bet,” Jillian said. “And a big hat and sunglasses sounds like a disguise to me. Like she was trying to keep her identity secret.”

Shelby snorted. “That's a horrible disguise. Everyone knows when you want to lie low you go with a ball cap.”

Jillian made a face. “Where'd you learn that from?”

“Literally any spy movie,” Shelby said, waving her off. “Anyway. Do you think she would have signed in at the front desk with her actual ID?”

“I mean…” Jillian sighed. She wasn't made for this private detective stuff. “Maybe. Though with Dad's money she could have easily gotten a fake. The real question is would they even have those kinds of records from over ten years ago? I mean, it's just a visitors' log.”

“You're probably right.” She clicked her tongue as they

signed out and made their way back to the car. "Maybe we should mention it to Hayes anyway? The private investigator can always chase the lead."

"I don't know if I'd call this a lead," Jillian remarked.

Shelby shot her an impatient look. "I mean…we're getting *somewhere…*"

"It just doesn't feel like we're any closer to learning the identity of the mystery heir," Jillian muttered as they got into the car. "Nick's going to run me by Dad's land tomorrow. I don't know what I'm hoping to find, but maybe inspiration will strike when I get there and I'll discover something about the connection between Dad and the land."

"Nick, huh?" Shelby teased.

"Don't say it like that."

Shelby checked her reflection in the mirror on the sun visor. "I didn't say it like anything."

"You *did*," Jillian insisted. "You have a tone."

"There's no tone," Shelby said, her voice far too even, far too calm. "It's just nice that he's taking you. That's all."

"He's the caretaker of the land," Jillian reminded her. "It's literally in the definition of the word. And what was he going to say, no? Of course he's taking me."

"Right." Shelby turned to Jillian, grinning wickedly. "How was dinner with him the other day?"

Jillian's heart skipped a beat. She hadn't even told her sister about that yet. "How did you—"

"Des," Shelby said. "He mentioned you'd stopped by to see Nick and Mandy the other night."

"When the hell did you talk to Des?" Jillian asked.

"He came by the house to drop something off for Mrs. Pulaski, and I answered the door. Apparently his mom's always baking up a storm. There were brownies, Jilly. *Amazing* brownies. Don't ask me how many I ate."

Jillian rubbed her eyes, sitting there in the parking lot. When had the ranch turned into one big gossip mill? And when the hell had her older sister become the center of it?

"So…how'd it go?" Shelby prompted again.

"Dinner was fine," Jillian admitted. "It was the kiss after—"

"You *kissed* him!" Shelby's eyes sparkled as Jillian flushed.

"Yes. Right there on his couch. And then I ran off."

"Jillian!" Shelby cried. "What? How?"

"I don't know," she stammered. "We were just talking, and the next thing I knew we were just…you know! But I pulled away and left because I didn't… He's not the usual guy I go for, and maybe he was just being nice and I misread the situation and—"

"Hey," Shelby said, clutching her hand. "Did you like it?"

"What?"

"Did you have a good time kissing Nick?"

"I… Yes," Jillian admitted even as she felt her cheeks flush with the heat of the sun.

"And did he have a good time kissing you back?"

"I think so," she said. He'd seemed into it right up until the point when she'd panicked and fled.

"Then it's not a *bad* thing," Shelby said. "Actually, this might be just what you need. Spend a little time with Nick and take your mind off all these dead ends."

Jillian hummed as she started the car, surprised that she didn't hate the idea. But even if she admitted that, did Nick think *she* was what *he* needed? Better yet, did he think she was right for Mandy? Their worlds were so different. It was hard to imagine that Nick would be interested in having her around when all she brought was a heap of family drama and daddy issues.

Nick and Mandy deserved better than that.

They deserved better than her, and that made her chest clench painfully.

Chapter Nine

"You're sure you have time to be doing this?" Jillian asked again as Nick unloaded supplies from the bed of his truck to the stables. She'd met him right at ten, like he'd asked her to, and when he'd walked around the end of his truck, dusting bits of straw from his fitted blue jeans… Well, maybe she'd stared a bit too long before realizing it. She was still fighting the heat of the blush she could feel running rampant across her face.

"I'm starting to think you don't actually want to go," Nick said, stopping to stare at her as he leaned against the back of the truck.

She crossed her arms. "That's not what I said. Of course I want to go, I just don't want to pull you away from anything important."

Lie.

If Jillian really examined herself, she'd see that she was looking for an excuse—*any excuse*—not to have to sit side by side with Nick Slater in his truck. Not to have to think about that night at his cabin and the way he'd fallen into her, head tilted, his kiss like fire.

"The land was important to your father, and it's my job to care for it," Nick said, cutting into her thoughts. "I'd be heading out there today with or without you to do my biweekly checks. So you're not pulling me away from anything."

"Mandy doesn't need you?" Jillian said.

"She's at preschool until three."

They hadn't been alone since they'd kissed, and her heart hammered at the thought, but she wasn't supposed to be thinking about any of that. She needed to stuff all of that confusion away because she was here for one reason: to find the heir. That was the only way to secure everyone's inheritance. To make sure their respective families were taken care of. To make sure she could continue to provide for King and the rest of the horses.

Nick smiled at her. Or was it more of a smirk?

She crossed her arms. "You're sure you don't want to resche—"

"Get in the truck, Jillian." Nick headed for the driver's door, and that left her no choice. Either stand there awkwardly or do as he said.

She headed for the passenger door and climbed inside. Nick started the engine and drove off the ranch, his truck bumping over gravel until he reached the main drive, which took them out to the stretch of highway that led to town. An hour east of Dallas, Emerald Ridge was the definition of affluence, nestled along the Emerald Ridge River. Most people referred to it as a Western resort town. It was famed for the popular Fortune's Gold Ranch, a legendary hot spring and a century-old, family-run winery that attracted visitors and VIP clientele from across the country. With the bustling two-mile long downtown stretch, Jillian had no idea why her dad had bought land all the way out past the railroad tracks. If he'd genuinely wanted to leave something to this potential heir, wouldn't it have made more sense to purchase land that was closer to downtown? Something that could be easily developed into a lucrative business?

She pondered that thought as Nick made his way through the downtown core.

"You're quiet," he said after a beat.

"Just thinking."

"About what?"

Not about you, she wanted to say because she was trying very hard to fend off the tension that was quickly engulfing the truck. Figuring out what that kiss meant would be so much simpler if she didn't live where Nick worked, if she wasn't so aware of his presence, if she wasn't suddenly looking for him on the ranch, *everywhere*. If she didn't *need* his help.

And she did need him.

So there was no choice.

Unless she was going to wrangle Shelby or one of her new siblings to follow this lead for her, but that felt foolish. She wasn't a little girl. She didn't have to run away and hide from her feelings.

She glanced at him.

He caught her eye for a brief moment, and in that space of time, his gaze seemed to smolder, his hair curled slightly at the ends from being pressed beneath his Stetson, his jaw shadowed with stubble.

Damn him for being so handsome.

And damn him again for making her feel like she was crushing on a boy for the first time ever.

"Well?" Nick prompted. "All this silence can't be good."

"I was just thinking about the land. Mostly wondering why my dad would have bought something all the way out here."

He shrugged. "Could be so many reasons. Expand the

business. Maybe he saw some future in commercial leasing. Tax write-off?"

Jillian shook her head. "I don't think it's any of that. Before my dad died, he left a letter with his attorneys to read, you know, in case it ever happened suddenly."

"The letter that told you about the bigamy?"

"Yeah, that one," she muttered. "The part that probably hasn't made its way through the rumor mill yet is that my dad had an affair."

Nick let out a low whistle. "Geez, Jillian, I'm so—"

"Hold on. There's more," she said, explaining as much as she knew about Lianna Dunhill and this supposed heir they had to track down. Nick shook his head, partly in shock, partly in disbelief.

"So the land is supposed to be for the heir?"

"If we can find them," Jillian clarified. "And I know the letter said the land was valuable, but I can't help thinking that if my dad wanted to set this heir up, the most economical opportunity would have been to buy something closer to downtown. It's going to cost a fortune to clear this land, never mind develop it if that's what this potential heir wants to do."

"Maybe he didn't mean *financially* valuable. Sure, the property is worth a lot, but maybe he was talking about another kind of value."

Jillian tilted her head, considering that. "My mother did say that Dad always refused to develop the land or sell it." She thought about the rest of the letter. "And Dad did write that the land held the key to his past. But we'd only discover what that was by becoming close to this supposed sixth sibling because they'd be inheriting the land."

"Dang, there are a lot of hoops for you to jump through, huh?"

Jillian massaged the space between her eyes. "I know. The attorneys were very specific. The five of us siblings have to work together to find the missing heir if we want our inheritance. And we literally have to detail *how* we work together."

The corner of Nick's mouth quirked. "You think the 'key to his past' part was literal or metaphorical?"

"I don't think we're going to dig up any buried treasure if that's what you're getting excited about."

"You never know," he mused. "There's a lot of land out here. Maybe one of you will be given a treasure map."

Jillian snorted. "I just don't understand why everything has to be so convoluted. Why didn't he look for this child if he wanted them to be a Fortune so badly? And why didn't he tell us any of this while he was still alive so we could ask him these things?" Frustration bubbled inside her, hot and frothy. It made her stomach ache.

"Maybe he always intended to," Nick said gently. "And then life got away from him."

Jillian huffed.

"Or…" he said. "Maybe he didn't know *how* to tell you when he was still alive. I can't imagine that would have been the easiest conversation. Plus, he was probably afraid of losing you all if he told the truth. I don't think anyone was ever going to take that news *well*."

Jillian swallowed hard. Could Nick be right? Maybe her dad had gotten so tangled up in his triple life that he didn't know how to unravel it without ruining everything. It certainly might have been the last straw for her. Whatever remained of their complicated relationship likely would have frayed with the revelation.

"Sometimes feelings are hard," Nick said gruffly. "That's what Mandy's counselor is always telling me. It's why we as humans go out of our way to do everything *but* what we actually want to do. Or say what we actually want to say."

Jillian arched her brow. "What are you getting at, cowboy?" He wasn't talking about the kiss was he?

"Nothing at all," he said, staring straight ahead. The truck rumbled over the railroad tracks. "Just that you might know a little about avoiding things."

Jillian straightened in her chair, scoffing at the look on his face. He *was* talking about the kiss! "Excuse me!"

"What?" he laughed. "*I'm* not the one who ran off."

"Hey, I was just making sure you didn't get too overwhelmed," she said.

Nick snorted, shaking his head. "Me? Really?"

"Not everyone can keep their cool in the presence of royalty."

"Okay, princess," he said. "I think maybe you're the one who got a little overwhelmed."

"By what?" she shot back. "All in all, it was a rather subpar kiss." He had to know she was lying, but she didn't care. She couldn't let him know how much it had really affected her.

Nick scoffed, his pitch rising. "I'm an *excellent* kisser!"

"Mmm..." Jillian hummed. "I'm holding out for the references to confirm."

"Ask the forty-nine stuffies I have to kiss every night before Mandy will go to sleep."

Jillian pretended to wince. "All that practice, and still only *okay*."

"Listen here, princess," Nick started.

Her lips twisted, trying to hold on to her smile.

He huffed, smiling back at her. "You're not allowed to give me a hard time. It's been a while."

"Oh, that's your excuse?"

"It is," Nick said. "And a perfectly valid excuse. But you know what they say."

"What?"

His eyebrow arched to a point as he glanced at her. "Practice makes perfect."

Jillian only *just* managed to hold on to the gasp that shot up her throat. She bit her lip, her stomach filled with butterflies at the thought of being close to him like that again.

"But speaking of visits to the cabin," he said, smoothly changing the subject. "Mandy would really like to see you again. She hasn't stopped talking about you since dinner."

"Really?"

"Well, it was about four words. But for Mandy—"

"Wow, she basically talked your ear off," Jillian teased. He laughed, and her heart fluttered at the sound.

"I've been a little worried about her lately, actually," Nick said, sobering. "So it's nice to see her a little more engaged."

"What about?" Jillian asked.

"She's been having a hard time making friends at school because she won't talk to the other kids."

"Oh, no." Jillian's chest tightened. She hated to think that after everything Mandy had been through, school would also be a difficult place for her.

"The other day when I went to pick her up," he said thickly, "a kid called her weird."

"I'm sorry, Nick. Kids can be mean at any age, I suppose. But especially when they're too young to understand things."

"I'm sure it bothered Mandy," Nick said. "Though it's not like it's easy for her to talk to me about it. It just sucks hearing the other kids say things like that. I've tried arranging playdates. My buddy Andrew has kids, but they're a little older than Mandy, and it's not the same thing as her making her own friends."

Jillian's heart broke for little Mandy, and not for the first time, she was moved by Nick's fierce commitment to caring for his niece.

"I just..." He shook his head, his jaw tight. "How much crap can one kid take?"

Jillian wanted to reach out and hug him, but he was driving, so she settled for putting her hand on his shoulder and squeezing. "You're a great uncle," she said. "And Mandy knows that. As long as she's got you as her safe space, everything else will get figured out."

"You think?" he asked quietly.

Jillian nodded. "I do."

"Thanks," he said, voice barely above a whisper. He cleared his throat, slowing the truck. "This is it."

Jillian hadn't even realized they'd arrived. There was no obvious signage like there was on the Fortune and Daughters Ranch. No big display announcing the mystery land belonged to Archibald Fortune. There was just a discreet wood-and-wire fence and a small gate, large enough for a vehicle to drive through. Nick hopped out of the truck to move the gate out of the way, then drove them down a worn track that carved through the property.

Once he parked before a copse of trees, Jillian got out to take it in.

"I usually head down this way," Nick said, "and do a bit of a walk. The property is too large to do a full perimeter check without a vehicle, but it's quiet out here. A nice place to come and think."

Water trickled nearby, and Jillian walked up a shallow hill to look over it. "Is that the Emerald Ridge River?"

"Yeah," he replied. "Cuts through the land. Not sure if the fishing is any good."

Jillian gave him a small smile then stared out at the water. "My dad requested that his attorneys scatter his ashes in the Emerald Ridge River. He didn't want a funeral."

"Maybe he didn't want all three of his families awkwardly fighting over the front pew in some church?" Nick offered.

"The attorneys said that he used to spend time at the river as a kid, net fishing to survive after his parents died. That it was a place of hope for him."

"I didn't know he was an orphan," Nick said.

"And I didn't know about the fishing thing," Jillian said, lifting her shoulder. "Because he never bothered to tell us any of these things while he was alive." Frustration flared inside her, and she knuckled that space between her ribs again.

Nick reached out, his fingers skimming her elbow. She looked at him. "Any theories?" he asked.

Jillian shook her head. "I think some ridiculous part of me actually thought I'd lay eyes on the property and then suddenly know what it was all about. But it's just trees and grass and the river… And really, he was around so infrequently, it feels like I barely knew the guy. And everything I *did* think I knew about him changed the day he died. So I don't know why I thought I'd suddenly have this epiphany or this great understanding of who my dad was." Tears burned behind her eyes, and her chest ached.

"Maybe the search for answers doesn't have to end here," Nick said softly.

She massaged her temple. "What?"

"We could look into a more detailed history of the land."

"*We?*" She dropped her hand and even smiled a bit, feeling a warmth spread through her belly.

"Well, you're trying to figure out this mystery. And for some reason, I'm caught up in it as the caretaker," Nick said. "So maybe I was always supposed to help you."

"I'd like that," Jillian told him. "Only I don't even know where to start."

Nick grinned. "I actually think I do."

Thirty minutes later, they pulled up in front of a squat brick building, the lettering on the large wooden door faded from the sun.

"The county clerk's office?" Jillian said.

Nick nodded, flicking his head toward the door. "Trust me. This is where the property records are kept."

She followed him inside, where fluorescents buzzed overhead. The building smelled of aged paper and wood polish. Behind a counter sat a receptionist, and behind her were rows of filing cabinets, desks cluttered with stacks of paper and half a dozen employees bent over files.

Nick walked up to the receptionist just as she hung up the phone. "Howdy," he said. "We'd like to look up some property information."

She produced a piece of paper. "Fill this request out with the address or parcel number."

Jillian watched as Nick scribbled it across the top of the page before pushing it back toward the receptionist.

"I'll pass this on to the public records department. Just have a seat please."

"Thank you," Nick said. They sat down in a pair of chairs against the far wall. They were small, hard plastic things, but Jillian didn't care. Her thoughts spun. What if they actually found something here?

"How'd you know to come here?" she asked as they waited to see if any records could be located.

Nick shrugged. "I had a buddy try to purchase some land once. When he finally got around to looking it up, it turned out it still belonged to the family of the original owner and couldn't technically be sold. Figured if there was anything to know, it'd be here. Might still be a long shot but—"

"It's a *shot*," Jillian finished for him, grateful to him for his help. "Thank you, Nick. I mean that."

He shrugged. "Had to kill some time before I go to pick up Mandy anyway."

Jillian chuckled as he flashed her a soft smile. The butterflies in her gut kicked up again. *Behave*, she told them, trying not to think about how nice it might be to take Nick by the collar and draw his lips to hers.

The receptionist cleared her throat. Nick and Jillian bounded to their feet. "This is all we have on that land," she said, tucking some papers into an envelope. "The clerk made photocopies for you."

"Thank you," Jillian said, retrieving the envelope and clutching it to her chest. It felt like she'd just been handed something fragile.

As they made their way back to the truck, her hands shook. "I'm almost afraid to open it," she admitted.

"You don't have to open it now."

"I want to," she said. "But I… I just want there to *be* something. You know?" She wanted answers of some kind. *Any* kind!

"How 'bout we go back to the cabin?" Nick offered. "I can grab Mandy on the way. Then we can see what's in there."

"Good idea."

They swung by the preschool to pick up his niece. Mandy's

eyes widened as she spotted Jillian, and she scrambled into the truck so quickly she dropped half her things. Then they made their way back to Nick's. He got Mandy settled on the couch with a snack and one of her shows, then he poured Jillian some sweet tea and they sat at the kitchen table.

"Ready?" he asked. She nodded. He pulled the papers from the envelope and laid them out in front of her, side by side.

Jillian's brow furrowed. "What is all of this?"

Nick scanned the documents. "Looks like historic land transactions, ownership details, property boundaries… Hey, wait, look at this." He shoved a piece of paper toward her. "A small parcel of the land your father bought was once owned by Clyde and Cass Fortune."

"*Fortunes?* When was that?" Jillian asked. This felt like the first real bit of information they'd found.

"Hmm…" Nick said, continuing to pore over the document. "About sixty-three years ago."

"And they sold it?"

He flipped the page over. "No, it looks like it was foreclosed on."

"Oh," Jillian said, wondering what had happened.

"Doesn't look like that part of the land is worth much on its own," Nick reported. "But the surrounding acres that your father bought up are what's worth the money."

"Who are Clyde and Cass?" Jillian mumbled under her breath. More importantly, who were they to her dad?

"Is there anyone you can ask?"

"Maybe my mom," Jillian said. "Though I'm sure she already would have said something if she knew anything about these people. Still, worth a shot. Thank you for all your help, Nick. Seriously."

"Of course."

Mandy stood up on the couch and banged her little bowl.

"I'm being summoned for more snacks," Nick said with a grin.

"And I should talk to my mom." For a beat, they just stared at each other. Jillian wanted to say more. Wanted to *do* more. Would it be weird to peck him on the cheek? Her heart skipped at the thought, but now was not the time. She forced herself to the door with all her papers.

"Let me know what she says," Nick said, walking her out.

Jillian nodded. "See you later?"

"Definitely."

Jillian waved goodbye to Mandy then hurried out the door to track down answers to her mystery.

Chapter Ten

"Mama?" Jillian called as she walked through the front door of the main house. Her voice carried across the foyer, echoing endlessly. "Mama, you in?" She'd spotted her car in the garage, so unless she'd gone out with a friend or with Shelby, there was a good chance that she was home.

"She's in the kitchen," Roxie, their housekeeper, said. She'd appeared at the top of the imperial staircase, descending one of the flights with a rag and a can of polish in her hand as Jillian removed her shoes. "Talking all things baby with Mrs. Pulaski."

"Of course she is," Jillian said, shaking her head fondly. Her mother had enthusiastically jumped into planning for her grandson's arrival the moment Shelby told them about the baby. Part of that, Jillian suspected, was to distract herself from the suddenness of losing Dad and learning about the bigamy. Honestly, Jillian couldn't blame her for throwing herself into wedding and baby planning. Her dad's deceit had rocked her hard; she couldn't even imagine what it was like for his wife. To have made vows to love and cherish and protect each other…and end up like this. "Thanks," she told Roxie before hurrying off to the kitchen.

When she arrived, the island had been cleared of dishware and flower vases and all manner of things to make room for the piles and piles of baby clothes. "Hey," she said, slightly overwhelmed.

"Hello, darling," Mama said, turning away from the counter to greet her. Agatha Fortune was a striking woman, even at sixty. Jillian had always thought she had a graceful, timeless beauty, with her soft features and warm brown eyes. Her dark hair, which Jillian had inherited, was now streaked through with touches of gray, but her smile remained that of a woman half her age. Mama held her arm out to Jillian, giving her a little squeeze.

Jillian pecked her on the cheek. She smelled like Chanel No. 5. "What's all this?" she asked.

"Everything," Mama said, standing next to Mrs. Pulaski. The two women stared at the piles of clothing. "But is it enough?"

"They grow quickly," their cook pointed out. "Could outgrow everything before they even have a chance to wear it."

"Yes, but you know Shelby," Mama said. "She'll have the little one in multiple outfits a day. And there are those days where you just can't seem to keep anything clean at all." Mama glanced at Jillian. "You were like that," she said. "Always spitting up everywhere. Couldn't take the burp cloth off my shoulder."

"Gee, that sounds lovely," Jillian muttered.

"Oh, you were a great baby other than that. And when we finally got your formula changed, you settled down. But there were days when I went through an entire drawer of sleepers."

"There *is* this thing called a washing machine," Jillian noted. "They even have a fifteen minute cycle nowadays."

"Sometimes it's easier just to leave them naked," Mrs. Pulaski said.

Mama hummed. "One more shopping trip can't hurt."

The other woman nodded in agreement before drifting back to the stove to stir something that smelled like her Emerald Ridge-famous tomato sauce.

"I feel like I haven't seen you in ages," Mama said. "Where have you been running off to lately?"

Agatha sat on one of the island stools, where she had a to-do list of baby essentials and wedding things written down. She could make a list like nobody's business. Jillian sank down on a stool of her own, placing the envelope with the papers from the county clerk's office down on the counter. "Madeline tracked down the caretaker of Dad's mysterious land, so I agreed to talk to him because he's one of our ranch hands."

For weeks after her dad passed, Jillian wasn't sure what to say to her mother. Despite his flaws and absences, it seemed that she'd really loved him, and Jillian hadn't thought it fair to dump all her anger toward Dad in her mother's lap. So she'd kept most things to herself, but now she had some questions.

"Oh, yes," Mama said. "That's right. Your sister mentioned you were catching a ride up to the property with him?"

Jillian nodded. "With Nick."

"Right, Nick Slater," Mama murmured, eyeing Mrs. Pulaski across the counter. "He's the one with the little girl?"

"That's Mandy, his niece."

"She's very cute."

"Adorable," Jillian agreed. "And very sweet."

"So..." Mama said, smiling at Jillian's words. "Any thoughts on the land? I always wondered what your father was holding on to it for. He'd just shrug it off when I asked, saying it was an investment for the future. I always assumed he meant *his* future and that he was looking to expand Fortune Air in some way. Maybe he'd build a factory of some sort or use it for storage. I never assumed he meant the future in terms of an heir." She sighed. "But I suppose I got used to not asking too many questions when it came to things like that."

"Why was that?" Jillian asked curiously. She leaned against the island and propped her head up with her hand.

"Well, I'd learned things about your father over the years, and I could tell when he didn't want to talk about something. There were topics that were hard for him. That brought up a lot of painful memories."

"Like about his childhood?"

Mama nodded. "He definitely didn't like to discuss that," she said. "In fact, he often refused. I think whatever he must have suffered as a child was partly why he was never fully able to give of himself as an adult, why he struggled to commit to people. I also think it's partly why he was so successful. He threw himself into his work, always jet-setting around the world to grow Fortune Air. But he carried a heaviness with him, and I always wished he would have let me help him with that."

Jillian tried not to scowl. Mama spoke of her dad's experience with such sadness and empathy. But Jillian still couldn't summon that same kind of compassion. She couldn't understand how Mama had seemingly moved past all his indiscretions so quickly. The lies. Marriages. The affairs. Not to mention all those secrets. Was love really enough to move on from all of that? Jillian swallowed hard. All she knew was that her childhood had been filled with its own questions: *Why did Dad miss Christmas again? Was he coming to see us off to school? Why didn't Dad show up for my riding competition? Why doesn't he love us enough to stay?*

After years, she'd simply stopped asking, stopped *expecting*, and the divide between her and her dad seemed to grow to an unbreachable place. And then he was just…gone.

"Well, I didn't learn anything from the land itself," Jillian explained. "I mean, it's nice for a walk especially with the river running through it, but it's sort of just this giant fenced-off acreage. But…" She pulled the papers from the envelope. "Nick had this idea to swing by the county clerk's office to look into the property records."

Mrs. Pulaski stopped stirring sauce and came to look over Mama's shoulder as Jillian laid out the documents. "Turns out that a part of the land that Dad bought used to belong to another set of Fortunes."

"Oh?" Mama said, picking up a page and scanning it.

"Do the names Clyde and Cass Fortune mean anything to you?" Jillian asked. She glanced from Mama to Mrs. Pulaski, seeing if the names registered with either of them. Mrs. Pulaski had been around this family and this town for a long time—so perhaps she'd heard of them somewhere.

Mama frowned while the cook shook her head.

"Dad never mentioned them to you?"

"No," Mama said. "Never. I definitely would have remembered those names if he had. I brought up the land so many times over the years."

"Do you think they could have meant something to him?" Jillian wondered. "Was that why he purchased this specific land or do you think it was just a coincidence?"

Mama drummed her lips with her fingers. "I honestly couldn't tell you, Jilly. I don't once remember your father ever mentioning anyone by the name of Clyde or Cass. But again, you know he rarely mentioned his past."

"I know." She sighed. It wasn't *quite* a dead end, but it wasn't the lead she was hoping for. Mrs. Pulaski drifted back to the stove. "I figured you'd already told us all you knew about the land, but I thought I'd ask anyway. I'll bring it up with Madeline and Hayes when Shelby and I see them next. They can check in with Damaris and Taffy. Maybe one of them have heard of Clyde or Cass."

"There are a lot of Fortunes in this town," Mrs. Pulaski remarked. "Someone will know who they are."

"Hopefully," Jillian said, carefully sliding the papers back into the envelope.

"Sorry I couldn't be more help, sweetheart." Mama took her hand and squeezed. "But I am very impressed with what you've learned so far. Shelby also mentioned you two went out to Bisonville to look into more about Lianna Dunhill."

"Also a bust," Jillian said.

"Well, I know this can't be easy. I'm proud of you for sticking with it."

"I don't imagine it's easy for any of us," Jillian said. "Dad really had to be difficult all the way to the grave."

"I don't think that's what he wanted," Mama countered, frowning a bit.

"Yeah," Jillian muttered. "That's what everyone keeps saying." She couldn't understand why everyone she knew kept giving Dad the benefit of the doubt. "But who actually knows what he wanted? He had three families and *still* none of us know." She sucked in a sharp breath, trying to keep her frustration from boiling over. "Sorry. I'm just… The answers are emerging slower than I'd like."

"I know, sweetheart." Her mother lifted her hand to cup Jillian's cheek. She leaned into the touch like she was a child again. "If you need to take a break from it—"

Jillian shook her head. "It's okay. I'm going to keep digging into Clyde and Cass around town. See if anything pops up that's useful." At this rate, she wasn't sure they'd ever find this mystery heir, but maybe Madeline or Hayes had had better luck unearthing something.

"Maybe a break is a good idea," Mrs. Pulaski suggested. "You could be spending more time with that handsome cowboy."

Jillian's entire face flushed. "Uh—"

Her mother's lips twisted like she was sitting on a secret, and Jillian suddenly suspected that she and Shelby had been discussing far more than just baby and wedding things.

"Yes, a little birdie tells me that you and Nick have been spending more than a little quality time together," Mama said.

"Was that birdie named Shelby?" Jillian grumbled. Shelby was going to get an earful the next time Jillian saw her. She could already imagine her sister's smug grin and hear her tinkling laugh as she said this was payback for all the times Jillian had read through her diary when they were teens.

"Maybe," Mama said.

Jillian crossed her arms. "Well, I don't know what she's talking about. *She* doesn't even know what she's talking about. Baby brain."

Mama eyed up Mrs. Pulaski again. "Mm-hmm," she said. "Are you sure there isn't something you'd like to tell me?"

Jillian arched a pointed eyebrow at her mother. Like what?

Like the fact that her heart raced every time she caught Nick's eye? Or how she couldn't stop thinking about the kiss they'd shared? How the more quality time they spent together, the harder it was to leave? Like the butterflies in her stomach had been dancing all day?

"Nope," Jillian said, brushing her off. "Not that I know

of." She was holding this card close to her chest until she knew what it really was. She didn't need Mama and Mrs. Pulaski and the rest of the dang ranch whispering about her and Nick. What if that scared him off? What if it scared *her* off?

She didn't even know what they were yet.

And she just…didn't want to ruin it. Plus, part of her didn't want to make her feelings into a big deal in case Nick wasn't feeling the same way. Despite his apparent interest in her, she still couldn't shake the memory of their first meeting, where he clearly saw some spoiled, snobby rich girl who couldn't tell one hired hand from the next.

Besides that, he was so worried about Mandy, and all Jillian could do was wax on about needing to secure everyone's inheritance and save her horses and… Did Nick look at her and see someone worthy of them? Or did he see her as a princess who couldn't possibly fit into their lives? If that was the case, she didn't need her heart any more tangled up than it already was.

"Mm-hmm," Mama said again, looking amused.

"When there's something to know," Jillian said. "*I'll* tell you. Until then, stop letting Shelby fill your head with nonsense."

"She—*we*—just want you to be happy, Jilly. It's been a rough time for everyone, and I think we all deserve a bit of that."

"I am happy," Jillian insisted, not wanting Mama to worry, but also realizing for the first time just how true that actually was. Despite all the inheritance drama lately and her complicated emotions regarding Dad, she was… content enough. Sure, she'd set her acting dreams aside at Archibald's insistence and she still had no idea what her purpose in life was, but she had a lot to be grateful for. "I've got my wonderful, nosy family," she teased, "and amazing friends and my volunteer work at the hospital."

And maybe I even have Nick, she thought. That brought a smile to her face.

She stood and pecked Mama on the cheek. "What more could a girl ask for?"

Chapter Eleven

"What time did they say they would be here?" Shelby asked, pressing her hand to her belly as they made their way into Francesca's Bar and Grill—the popular family-run restaurant located in downtown Emerald Ridge.

"Noon," Jillian said, holding the front door open for her sister. It had been a few days since she'd been to the county clerk's office with Nick, and though she hadn't come up with any more info on Clyde and Cass Fortune just yet, she was pleased to be able to pass on the information she *did* have.

"Good," Shelby announced, inhaling deeply as they entered the restaurant. She groaned. "I'm starving."

"You're *always* starving." They'd opted for lunch because the dinner rush was often so packed Jillian could hardly hear herself think, but the burgers were to die for, and Madeline and Hayes were still finding their feet in town. As the resident sisters, Jillian felt it was their duty to show their new siblings the best of what Emerald Ridge had to offer. Though even as she thought that, her mind turned to Nick and Mandy. To burgers at the cabin and kisses on Nick's couch. And she knew immediately that anything Francesca's had to offer would pale in comparison to that meal.

"I know." Shelby checked her phone. "Okay, we're a little early. That gives me time to pee."

"You just went at the house," Jillian said as she walked up to the hostess.

"*I* know that and *you* know that. But this baby does not care." Shelby veered off down a hallway to use the bathroom. Jillian rolled her eyes, chuckling under her breath. Every day she learned some new, fascinating—and sometimes horrifying—tidbit about pregnancy.

"Hello," the hostess said. She was young, with pin-straight blond hair and a cheery smile. "Can I help you?"

"We have a reservation," Jillian said. "Under Shelby."

"Oh, yes, I have you here. One of your party has already arrived. I'll take you through."

Jillian followed the girl to a booth near the back of the restaurant, spotting a now familiar head of red hair. Madeline Fortune, her new half sister and daughter of the prickly Taffy Fortune, had thankfully inherited none of her mother's special brand of...*charm*. She was warm and kind and always greeted Jillian and Shelby with a big smile.

She looked up from her phone, where she seemed to be engrossed in an email, her bright green eyes locking on Jillian's. Madeline ran Let's Get This Party Started—an event planning business that Jillian knew kept her busy, especially now that she was looking for a place to set up shop on Central Avenue. Moving the business from Dallas to Emerald Ridge was proving to be a bit of a headache, but considering they were in the middle of the hunt for the missing heir, it seemed more sensible to Madeline to try to put down roots in town. Jillian was glad to have her and Hayes around. With Shelby so often occupied by baby and wedding things, it was nice to have some other minds to bounce ideas and frustrations off of.

"Hey, you," Madeline said, stepping out of the booth to give Jillian a hug. As Madeline wrapped her arms around Jillian, it still astonished her how two people could be so different. During the meeting with the attorneys, it quickly became clear that Taffy Fortune was a vindictive and angry woman, outwardly seeming to hate Archibald. And though Jillian couldn't exactly blame her after his betrayal, the true animosity became clear when Taffy suggested that she wanted nothing to do with any of his other wives or *spawn*. Thankfully, Madeline had been more receptive to the terms of the will, otherwise getting this matter of inheritance sorted would be a lot more complicated.

"Hey," Jillian said, giving her a quick squeeze in return. She still didn't always know how to greet her new siblings. It was like meeting relatives you hadn't seen all year, except it had actually been an entire lifetime. Did they hug? High five? Awkwardly fist bump? Thankfully, Madeline usually took the lead, making it less awkward, and maybe one day they'd feel more like actual sisters than weirdly distant relatives. "How are things?"

"Busy," she admitted. "I've been viewing potential storefront locations all week. But I'm excited to get the ball rolling. And happy for the excuse to get away from all the planning for a while and have lunch."

Jillian imagined she was especially busy now that Madeline was planning Kate Fortune's one hundredth birthday—the mogul behind Fortune Cosmetics. "Honestly, weeding through paperwork on the mysterious land is confusing enough—I don't know how you keep all those planning details organized."

Madeline laughed. "Sometimes I don't know myself. I make a lot of lists."

"You and my mother would get along well," Jillian said.

Her half sister slid back into the booth, and Jillian slid in beside her. "Shelby not coming?"

"Oh, she's here. She had to stop by the ladies' room," Jillian said. "Apparently the baby is sitting on her bladder or something."

Madeline chuckled. "Yikes."

"You can say that again," Shelby said, wandering up to the table with Hayes, their new brother, in tow. Well…*one* of them. They hadn't actually met his brother Penn yet. "Look who I found waiting in the lobby."

"Hey, y'all," Hayes said. He was tall, with brown hair and blue eyes, and was always in a Stetson. At first glance the former champion bronc rider didn't strike Jillian as anything like Archibald, but then he'd remove his hat and the light would hit him just right, and she would see flashes of their dad. It unsettled her, mostly because it tugged on a part of her that missed him, and she hated that. Hayes shot her a tight smile. They'd quickly come to realize that they'd both had a strained relationship with Archibald, never feeling particularly close to him, and that had created an immediate bond.

"Doing okay?" Jillian asked him.

"Yeah." He let out a sigh that suggested otherwise as he and Shelby sat down. Once everyone had perused the menu, the four of them ordered drinks and appetizers to start.

"So, updates," Shelby said, setting her menu aside. "We went to speak to Lianna Dunhill's elderly aunt."

"The one out in Bisonville?" Madeline asked.

Shelby nodded. "Turns out she wasn't much help in the end."

"Why not?" Hayes prodded.

"She's living in the memory care ward at a ritzy nursing home," Jillian explained. "She's got dementia, and though she lit up at the mention of Lianna, we didn't really get anything useful out of her." Besides the fact the birds needed more seeds. "It'd be very unlikely that she'd be able to tell us anything, even if we kept visiting."

"Darn," Madeline said. "That's a bummer."

The waitress returned with their drinks. When she was gone, Jillian said, "But on a positive note, one of the nurses did mention that a woman used to visit Jeralyn until about ten years ago."

"Right around the time Liana passed?" Hayes said, making a note for himself in a small notepad. He was always jotting things down for the private investigator.

"Seems like it," Shelby said. "And she apparently always turned up disguised with big hats and sunglasses."

Madeline frowned. "That sounds like a woman doing a horrible job of trying to stay under the radar."

"That's what I said!" Shelby cried.

Madeline wrinkled her nose. "What kind of spy movies was she watching?"

"Thank you!"

Jillian rolled her eyes in amusement at the two of them. "Don't encourage her detective skills."

"I'll let the private investigator know," Hayes said.

"Oh, we did wonder if she might have used her ID to sign in at reception," Jillian said. "We both had to when we arrived."

"And we were thinking that maybe there will be some sort of records on file that the PI could request?" Shelby chimed in.

Hayes nodded, adding more to his notebook. "The PI is still looking into the restaurant Lianna worked at when she met Dad. I'll give him the tip, and hopefully we'll get some more concrete answers soon."

The waitress returned with their appetizers, and they cleared room on the table.

"Speaking of more concrete answers," Jillian said, grabbing a truffle fry and nudging Madeline. "I've been looking into the land Dad intended to leave the sixth heir with Nick Slater."

Shelby eyed her across the table, a tiny smirk on her lips, but Jillian ignored her because she wasn't prepared to get into *that* right now.

"What did you find out?" Madeline asked. Her face fell suddenly. "Or was it another dead end?"

"Yes and no," Jillian said. "Turns out a small parcel of the land once belonged to a couple by the name of Clyde and Cass Fortune."

"And they are?" Hayes inquired.

"Exactly," Jillian said. "I'm not sure. I asked our mother, but she had no idea, either. You two haven't heard those names before, have you?" Madeline shook her head. Hayes scribbled the names down in his book, and Jillian took that as a no. "I was thinking you could check in with your moms? See if it ever came up in their conversations with Dad. I'll keep looking into the names around town, though."

"Sounds good," Hayes said, rubbing at his eyes.

"You look tired," Shelby noted. "Getting enough sleep?"

"Honestly," he huffed, "probably not."

"What's on your mind?" Madeline asked him.

His eyebrows twitched like he was trying not to frown. "I'm a little worried about Penn."

"He still won't budge?" Jillian questioned. So far, Penn had refused to come to Emerald Ridge or to work with them to fulfill the terms of the will. If they couldn't get him on board, everyone's inheritance was at risk. But what could the rest of them do other than trust Hayes to convince his brother to do the right thing?

Hayes shook his head.

"Why not?" Shelby demanded. "Has he said?"

"Not really," Hayes offered with a shrug. "He just keeps giving me the runaround. But I've put it on the list of things to get to the bottom of."

"Feels like that list keeps getting longer," Madeline said.

"Tell me about it," Hayes muttered. He shifted in his seat, looking uncomfortable, then glanced down at his watch. "If those are the updates, I've actually gotta get going..."

"*Already?*" Shelby said, looking a little disappointed. Jillian could understand. It might be silly, but having a brother—even a half brother—was a bit of a novelty for them. "Not gonna stay for the main course?"

"Nah. I'll catch up with you guys later, though," Hayes promised. "And I'll keep you posted if the PI comes through with any other info." He got to his feet, tucked his Stetson back on his head and left.

Jillian stared after him and hummed.

"What is it?" Shelby asked, catching her look.

Jillian leaned toward them, keeping her voice low. "Didn't he seem off to you?"

"Well, yeah," Shelby replied. "He said himself that he's not sleeping great."

"I know," Jillian said, "but I wonder if there's more to this Penn thing than he's actually telling us."

"Like what?" Madeline interjected. "Some sort of family secret?"

Jillian bit her lip. She thought back to that day last month when all three families had been brought together by the attorneys at the Emerald Ridge Hotel. Hayes and his mother

Damaris had turned up without Penn. "Remember how nervous Damaris was at the meeting with the lawyers?"

"More than nervous," Madeline said thoughtfully. "At one point Damaris looked downright uncomfortable. My mother couldn't stop talking about it after we left."

Of course Taffy had picked up on it. "Well," Jillian continued, "something is clearly going on with them. I just..."

"What?" Shelby asked, nose wrinkling at her tone.

"I just hope it isn't something that's going to end up hurting us all," Jillian said. "I for one have had more than enough with all the secrets."

"Agreed," Madeline murmured. "Maybe it'll take them some time, but hopefully, whatever it is, Hayes will come around to telling us eventually."

"I think we deserve at least that," Shelby agreed.

Jillian sucked in a heavy breath and released it. Why did everything have to be so complicated?

"In other news, want to hear the latest party planning drama?" Madeline said, making Jillian and Shelby smile as they worked their way through the rest of their appetizers. "You know how I'm arranging Kate Fortune's hundredth birthday party for July?"

Shelby nodded. "Yeah?"

"Well, she called me today, out of the blue, and said that a very special guest *must* be in attendance at her party or there might as well not even be a party at all."

"That's...intense," Jillian remarked. "And this wasn't a requirement when you first spoke?"

Madeline shook her head. "But get this, it turns out that Kate's long-estranged great-great-grandniece is none other than Susannah Simmons!"

"*Hold on*," Shelby said, throwing her hands down on the table. "You mean like the famous actress, Susannah

Simmons?" Shelby reached across and snatched Madeline's hand. "The one who disappeared from the spotlight last year amid all those rumors? I read about all that in the tabloids!"

"She was obsessed," Jillian noted. "There were magazines all over the house."

"Well," Madeline said with a small smile. "Word has it that she lives in a remote luxe ranch in Emerald Ridge and goes out only in disguise."

"*Ohhhh*, what?" Shelby said. "This whole time?"

"Yep," Madeline confirmed.

Shelby's jaw dropped. "The drama! The mystery! The intrigue!"

Jillian rolled her eyes. "This isn't one of your soaps, Shelb. Calm down."

Shelby waved her off. "Do you know what caused the estrangement? Did Kate say anything? I need details..."

Madeline shook her head. "No, Kate wouldn't say anything about that, and I didn't feel right prying."

"Girl!" Shelby exclaimed. "Next time you get Kate Fortune on the phone, call me, and *I* will pry."

"She totally will," Jillian said. "It's one of her special talents. Do you think you can get Susannah to come to the party?"

Madeline sighed. "Well, right now I can't even get a number for Susannah, and if she does really live in that luxe remote ranch, she doesn't answer her door." She shrugged. "But I'll have to keep trying. This party is a big deal. It could literally make or break my business here in Emerald Ridge, so I need it to be perfect. And besides that, I could hear in Kate's voice how much it means to her to have Susannah attend. So somehow I have to make this happen. No time for disasters."

"You can say that again," Shelby said, and Jillian couldn't help but feel she was talking about more than just this party.

Chapter Twelve

"Hey there, cowboy," a gentle voice called, and Nick's pulse skipped before he'd even turned around.

When he did, he spotted Jillian walking down the center aisle of the stables—which, aside from Mandy's smile, had quickly become one of his favorite sights in the world. He didn't want to be too presumptuous, thinking she was only out here because of him, but the frequency of her visits had seen a sharp uptick in the past couple of weeks. That was all Nick was gonna say. Today she was clad in a fitted, long-sleeved cream shirt under a black vest, form-fitting pants that made his gaze linger longer than it should on her legs and riding boots.

"Taking King out?" he asked, dragging his gaze back to her face, where it was safe.

"I was thinking about it," she said, giving him a soft smile. "Are you on your lunch break?"

He nodded. He was sitting on a hay bale, finishing up the sandwich he'd packed himself. He usually went home for chow in between rounds of chores, but sometimes when there were extra chores to do around the stables or deliveries being made, he brought his lunch with him to save time. "What have you been up to today?"

"*Ughhh*," Jillian said, grumbling in the back of her

throat. "I've been at the house, poring over the paperwork from the county clerk's office all morning. I think my eyes have shriveled up into raisins."

Nick laughed. "Not going well?"

She sighed and slumped down on the hay bale beside him. Her shoulder bumped his, and he leaned into the contact, enjoying the warmth of her presence. "I mean, no worse than it *has* been going," Jillian admitted. "I met with all the siblings yesterday to update them on the progress with the land."

"What'd they say?"

"Hayes has hired a private investigator, so he's going to pass on all the information he can. But Hayes and Madeline had never heard the names Clyde or Cass Fortune. My mother didn't seem to know anything, either, so that leaves Damaris and Taffy. My hopes aren't high considering they've never even lived in Emerald Ridge, but maybe they managed to get more information out of my dad over the course of their relationships."

"How are *you* doing?" Nick asked pointedly. He could hear the edge of frustration in her voice despite the small smile she offered him. It was enough to send blood pulsing through his veins, and his hand itched to reach for her, to tangle their fingers together between them. He liked the way she was looking at him right now. And that she felt safe enough to confide in him about her struggles.

"I guess I'm okay," Jillian said. "But I think I'll be better when we track down this heir and put this whole mystery to bed. I'm not cut out for these endless unanswered questions."

"Shelby and the baby okay?"

Jillian nodded. "She's in full wedding and nesting mode.

And she's trying her best to help out with the will and stuff, but her mind's definitely elsewhere most of the time."

"I'm sure that gets a little frustrating," Nick said.

"There are moments," Jillian admitted. "But then I remind myself that I'd rather her be happy and content and excited about the future instead of stuck in the past, where I seem to be."

"You're a good sister," Nick rumbled, nudging her shoulder. "Shelby's lucky to have you."

Jillian nudged him back until they sort of rocked together, then she reached out and caught his hand, threading their fingers together. A surge of heat spread through Nick as he tightened the hold, his calloused palm pressing against her smooth skin. He thought back to that night they'd kissed. And he thought about how much he wanted to pull her close now, to hold her. If he kissed her again now, would she spook? Did she want him as much as he wanted her?

Their eyes met, but Jillian's expression was unreadable.

"Sometimes," she said.

"What?"

"Sometimes I'm a good sister." She tilted her head, eyes twinkling. "I've done my duty as a little sister and given her hell a lot of the time, so I should occasionally be nice. Plus with Madeline and Hayes around, it's not like I'm completely on my own trying to solve this." She stared down at their entwined hands, and Nick stared at her. "I mean, Madeline does have her party business, and she's currently planning Kate Fortune's one hundredth birthday party, which is keeping her pretty occupied. And Hayes is busy trying to figure out what's going on with his brother, who seems to be avoiding Emerald Ridge at all costs. So I guess in some ways a lot of this is falling on me, but I suppose that just says I have nothing else going on in my life right now."

"That's not true," Nick said.

Jillian's eyes lifted. "It is, though. Madeline's brought her business to Emerald Ridge, and Hayes has his company. Even Shelby is working on starting up her own enterprise in the middle of planning for a baby and a wedding. And I'm just..." She sighed. "Not quite sure what I'm doing. Or what I'm *supposed* to be doing."

"Hey," Nick said, running his thumb over her knuckles. "I don't think anyone's expecting you to figure that out right now."

"Maybe not anyone, but *I'm* starting to expect something more of myself," Jillian admitted. "Losing my dad so suddenly has made me realize that I never figured out my thing. And I don't want to spend the rest of my life brunching with Melissa and Rory."

"You never had hopes and dreams of doing something?" Nick asked.

"Oh, I was full of hopes and dreams."

"Like?"

"You know," Jillian said, giving him a wan smile, "the usual things little girls want to do."

"Princess?" Nick asked.

Jillian nodded. "Astronaut. Pizza chef. Mermaid."

"Maybe you oughta cut yourself some slack," Nick said. "I hear the mermaid bizz is tough to break into."

Jillian laughed uncertainly. "Feels like I've been cutting myself too much slack lately. Anyway, enough of my existential dread, what've you got on the agenda for the rest of today?"

"I don't mind listening to your existential dread," Nick murmured.

"And I appreciate that." She bumped him, raising her eyebrow, waiting for an answer.

"Almost done with chores," he told her. "I just have to turn one more horse out. Then I have to pick Mandy up from school in a couple of hours. Apparently, she's gotta bring one hundred of something into class tomorrow to celebrate them learning to count to one hundred. So Mandy and I have to figure that out tonight."

"I remember doing that," Jillian said, chuckling. "It's funny how some of these activities don't change no matter how many years pass."

"Well, if you have any ideas, I'm all ears." Nick blew out a breath. "I don't know if we own one hundred of *anything* despite how often Mandy tries to get me to buy her more stuffed animals." Unless of course dog hair counted because Otto was constantly shedding up a storm.

"I think when Shelby and I did it way back in the day, Mrs. Pulaski helped us both bake one hundred cookies," Jillian told him. "Maybe it was cheating a little, but they sure were delicious and beat having to put one hundred pennies in a jar."

"That's…actually a great idea," Nick told her. "And if I could bake at all, that's totally what we'd be doing tonight."

Jillian released his hand and climbed to her feet, shooting him a grin. "Well, cowboy, lucky for you, I *can* bake."

"Really?" he said, collecting his garbage from lunch. "The woman with a private chef can bake?"

Jillian scoffed. "Mrs. Pulaski's not just a chef. She's family. And she *insisted* that Shelby and I know the basics of cooking so we could survive college. So, yeah, I'm not gonna be making you any Michelin-star meals, but I can manage some chocolate chip cookies."

"I'll have to see it to believe it," Nick retorted. He stood even as his mind got caught on her words about making him a Michelin-star meal—or rather *not* making it. The way she'd said it felt like they were talking about a future where they might do that kind of thing together, and he liked the sound of that. He also liked the thought of a future with her, in whatever form it came, and it made his head spin. Maybe it was dangerous to be thinking that way already, but he couldn't help himself.

"All right, then. You can bring Mandy by the house tonight, and I will show you my chocolate chip cookie baking skills."

Nick cocked his head to the side. "You're serious?"

"I am."

His pulse skittered at the thought of spending the evening with her. "Sure we won't be imposing or anything?"

"No." She tucked her arms against her chest, her lips quirking. "But you will forever be in my debt, Nick Slater."

He smirked. "How can I ever repay you?"

She gestured to the tack that hung over the nearest gate with her chin. "By coming for a ride with me."

"*Now?*" Nick said.

"When else?" Jillian turned and hauled the tack off the gate. "Get saddled up, cowboy!"

Twenty minutes later, they were out on the trail beyond the pastures, Jillian on King and Nick on the gray Andalusian they called Buck as they headed into a tiny copse of trees. The canopy above was still sparse after winter, leaving a trail of sun-dappled shadows ahead of them.

Jillian trotted ahead, her posture relaxed, laughing freely as King jumped a small branch that had fallen across the trail.

"Show-off," Nick said as he guided his horse around it.

He was old enough to know better than to attempt tricks he had no business doing.

Jillian beamed at him. "That was barely a jump."

He arched his brow.

"Okay, it was a little jump," she conceded. "But I'm a professional."

"You used to jump?" he said. He should have known just by her posture alone.

"Oh yeah, competitively." Jillian shook her head. "It was my entire personality for a while."

Nick flicked his reins, urging his horse ahead to catch up with her. "How many years did you compete?"

"I started around twelve," Jillian said, leading her horse around a puddle, "after years of riding and training for show jumping." She tilted her head back, smiling like she was reliving a fond memory. "It was everything to me."

Nick chuckled.

"What?" she asked.

"Nothing. I'm just imagining little Jillian, in her helmet and show jacket. Serious face on." He squinted as a ray of sun cut across his face, and he tipped his hat forward. "The quintessential horse girl."

Jillian laughed. "I *was* that girl."

"Sounds like you really loved it."

"I did," she said. "For a while. And then somewhere along the way I fell out of love with it. I hung up my show jacket when I was about seventeen."

"What changed?" Nick wondered. How did you go from loving something so much to simply not caring about it anymore?

Jillian hummed. "Not sure," she said. "Don't get me wrong, I still love riding and I love the horses, but I think at that time I mostly loved the idea of having a *thing*. Shelby had pageants and she excelled at them, and I just wanted something to throw myself into so I didn't have to think about Dad and why he didn't seem to want to spend any time with us. Then I realized I was pretty good at it—the show jumping—and I threw myself into it. I ate, slept, and breathed jumping. It was a good distraction for a while, but the better I did, the more I expected to see Dad there in the stands, sitting next to Mama and..."

"He never was?" Nick guessed. He couldn't imagine not being there for something Mandy was doing, to support her and cheer her on no matter how well she did in the end.

Jillian's smile thinned. "That's how the story goes. But I do still have some fond memories and a neat party trick now."

"Not sure it works well at parties," Nick said, shooting her a warm smile.

"No, but it was enough to impress you."

"After show jumping, was there nothing else you liked doing?" he asked.

"Actually," Jillian said, flushing a bit. "I sort of had an acting thing for a while."

"Wait, really?"

She nodded. "I did this stage-management program at my school and absolutely fell in love with it. All the behind-the-scenes work. All the on-stage drama, so to speak. When I first tried acting, I didn't think I'd like it. Standing in front of a crowd and having all those eyes on me..." She pretended to shiver. "But I did my first small speaking role, and it was exhilarating. There was something freeing about getting to be a completely different person."

Their horses drifted closer together, matching pace. Nick could hear the joy in her voice. "Why aren't you still acting then?"

She scoffed, shaking her head. "Dad shut it down. Said it was a waste of my time. He never came to any of my shows, and back then, I wondered if I embarrassed him. That was enough to kill my desire to be on stage. Now, though, I'm starting to wonder if he was protecting his secret."

"Like he was worried you'd out him if you ended up on the big screen somewhere?" Nick asked.

"Can't have your daughter's name up in lights if you're trying to conceal secrets about your own," she said. "Anyway, since then I've always sort of felt like I was drifting career-wise, trying to figure out my niche."

Nick blew out a strangled breath. "That's really crap, Jillian. I'm sorry you didn't get the support you needed."

"I got used to things being crap when it came to Archibald." She shrugged it off, but Nick couldn't quite let it go. He hated to think that Jillian had second-guessed something she loved doing all because Archibald couldn't spare the time to show any interest in her.

His hands tightened around the reins as he vowed to always support Mandy in whatever she wanted to do. Cheerleading? He'd be there in the crowd, yelling the loudest. Chess club? He'd read up on all the strategies to make sure he was a worthy opponent. Computer programing? Hell, he'd buy her all the gadgets and learn to code if that's what it took to support her.

"Hey, look!" Jillian said, pulling his attention as she nodded ahead. "Shelby and I used to play out here all the time when we were kids. We'd run off and hide from the au pair and build forts in the woods. Used to drag Mama's good blankets out here and get an earful about that."

Au pair? It was a strange word to his ear. Nick tried to imagine what it would be like to hand Mandy over to a babysitter all day. As stressed as he sometimes was running her back and forth to school and the hospital with work thrown on top, he wouldn't trade those moments with her for anything. Each time he looked in the rearview mirror and saw Mandy smiling back at him, he also saw his brother and his sister-in-law in equal measure, and it made that hole in his chest feel a little less hollow. But Jillian had grown up in a different world from him. One where she was handed over to a stranger and told to behave. One with boarding schools and fancy galas. Nick didn't think he would ever understand it, and there were moments when he worried he'd never quite understand *her*, like they'd always walk slightly out of step with one another. But right now, out here, sharing space on the same quiet trail, they didn't feel out of step.

They felt…connected.

Lately, Jillian was the only one he wanted to spend time with. He thought about her when he woke up in the morning and again before he went to sleep. He fixated on her smile and what he might say to get her to laugh and how he might entice her to hold his hand again. Nick was falling under her spell, hard and fast, his desire to hold her close growing stronger by the moment. Mostly, he thought about what it would be like to kiss her again. To *really* kiss her, with no hesitation or fear. He wanted a real one, not some fumbled thing on the couch in his cabin.

"This was a good idea," he remarked as they emerged on the other side of the trees, a meadow rolling out ahead of them filled with prickly grasses and the first bluebonnets of spring. Nick sucked in a deep breath of fresh air.

"Thanks for riding with me," Jillian said.

"Thanks for inviting me."

"You're always invited," she murmured. The horses

slowed almost to a standstill. Jillian twisted in her saddle to look at him head-on. "I want you here with me, Nick."

"Yeah?"

She nodded, her words soft as she whispered, "Yeah."

Nick's gaze dropped from her eyes to her lips, and the next thing he knew, she was tipping toward him.

He tilted his head to capture her lips. The kiss was gentle, fleeting, their horses bumping against each other, the angle awkward, but Nick didn't care. All that mattered was Jillian's giddy little smile as she pulled away.

"Not gonna run off on me again, are you?" he rasped.

"No," she answered, her smile turning wicked. "But I am gonna race you to the fence out there. Loser has to do the dishes tonight!" She kicked her heels hard, and King shot off like a rocket, his flowing tail blowing in the breeze.

"That's cheating!" Nick called after her. He clicked his tongue and kicked hard, laughing as his Stetson almost blew off his head.

Nick followed Mandy around Jillian's giant kitchen, afraid that she was going to put her grubby, flour-dusted hands on something important. He was sure some of these dishes cost more than his monthly salary and he wasn't prepared to be replacing them. Frankly, he thought they were supposed to be making cookies, but instead all they were making so far was one hell of a mess.

Jillian laughed and pointed a wooden spoon at him. "Just relax. She's having fun."

"That's what I'm worried about. I'm afraid she's gonna mess something up." The counter in this place sparkled more than the diamond in his mother's engagement ring.

"It's a kitchen," Jillian said, licking a bit of batter off the end of her finger. "It's *supposed* to get messy."

As his eyes drifted from one end of the massive room to the other, he realized suddenly that his entire cabin could fit in here. It made him uneasy, not because he had any issue with his position in life, but because he liked Jillian a hell of a lot and *this* was what she was used to. Nick would never be able to afford a place like this or measure up to the likes of what Archibald Fortune had been able to accomplish in his life. He knew that like he knew that the sun would rise in the morning, and part of him worried that maybe when the novelty of their feelings wore off, Jillian would come to that same conclusion. But for now all she did was smile at him from across the counter.

"Oh, something smells lovely!" Agatha Fortune walked into the kitchen carrying handfuls of shopping bags.

"Mama," Jillian complained. "*More* baby clothes?"

"I just saw a couple cute things while I was out," she said, grinning as she placed the bags on the other end of the island where they'd be safe from Mandy's sticky fingers and the copious amounts of flour that had gotten everywhere. "Hello, Nick."

He nodded in her direction. "Mrs. Fortune. Nice to see you."

She rolled her eyes at him in a way that was so similar to Jillian it made him grin. "Agatha, please."

Nick hadn't exactly had much interaction with the matriarch of the family, but he knew who she was, and she obviously knew him well enough to know his name. He wondered if Jillian had something to do with that.

"And who's this little angel?" Agatha said, looking at Mandy.

Mandy touched her chest but didn't say anything.

"This is Mandy," Jillian said sweetly, though he suspected Agatha already knew that, too. "We're making one hundred cookies for her to take to school tomorrow."

"Oh, I remember when you girls did that." She eyed the wire racks where cookies cooled. "I hope there are a couple left over. I bet Shelby would love to give them a try."

Jillian snorted. "We will definitely be hiding these from Shelby. Or else Mandy will turn up with seventy-five cookies instead of one hundred."

Agatha laughed. "You know what?" she said. "I bet we have some of Shelby's very first pageant costumes put away in storage. Some of them are probably just about Mandy's size. I'm going to go see if Roxie knows where they are."

"Not sure I'm ready for pageants," Nick muttered to Jillian as Agatha hurried from the kitchen. "I'm barely keeping up with the pigtails."

Jillian and Nick both looked down to Mandy's slightly skewed hair.

"True," Jillian said. "You're awful at it."

"Hey!" Nick replied, grinning at the teasing look on her face.

"I'm kidding. I know you're doing the best you can. You better just hope you improve before Mandy realizes your best isn't very good."

Nick huffed. "I'll have you know I'm getting better every day." His phone started buzzing in his pocket. He pulled it out. "*My* mother," he said to Jillian. "You mind if I—"

"Go for it," Jillian replied, letting Mandy dump an entire bag of chocolate chips into a bowl and attack them with a wooden spoon.

Nick answered the video call. "Hey," he said before turning the phone in Mandy's direction. He knew his mother was mostly calling to talk to her. "Say hi to Grandma, Squeaks."

Mandy beamed at the phone, giving her a chocolatey smile. She'd clearly been sneaking more chocolate chips than she was actually getting in the cookies.

"What'cha got there?" his mother asked.

"Cookies!" Mandy announced so loud it surprised both him and Jillian. They exchanged a pleasantly surprised look.

"Cookies?" his mother replied. "They look delicious. Are you going to save some for Grandma?"

The little girl nodded.

"She's lying through her teeth," Nick said, laughing as he turned the phone back on himself. "Jillian was kind enough to help us make one hundred cookies to celebrate Mandy's class learning the numbers from one to one hundred this month."

"Oh, that's the girl you were telling me about," his mother said. "The one you said you couldn't stop—"

Good Lord! Nick swapped the call from video to voice and took the phone off speaker, pressing it to his ear. "Ma, c'mon," he complained. Did parents really never outgrow the need to embarrass their kids?

"What?" his mother said.

"We'll call you before bed so you can say good-night," Nick said, almost afraid to let his gaze drift back to the other end of the kitchen as embarrassment flooded his veins.

His mother snorted. "Give Mandy my love."

"Always do. Talk later." Nick hung up.

When he turned around, Jillian was forming cookie dough balls, trying not to smile. "You told your mom about me?" she said, her voice even.

"Maybe. You told yours about me?"

"Maybe," Jillian replied cheekily.

They stared at each other, tension coiling around them. Nick wanted to cross the room and grab hold of her with both hands, the mess be damned, and—

"*Did it!*" Mandy declared, effectively ending the moment.

"You did!" Jillian said, looking down at Mandy's tray. "I think that's gonna be the best cookie so far. What do you think, Uncle Nick?"

Nick walked over and glanced down at the mashed mound of dough she'd slapped down on the baking sheet. It sorta looked like a bunch of horse droppings if he was being honest. And judging by the way Jillian bit her lip, he suspected she might be thinking the same exact thing. Mandy stared up at him expectantly, blinking those adorably blue eyes at him. So he did the only thing he could and lied. "I've never seen a better cookie in my life, Squeaks!"

Chapter Thirteen

"Okay, this place is kind of cute," Melissa said as they walked up a flight of stone steps into the interior of the building. High vaulted ceilings soared above them, and arched windows allowed streams of natural light to bathe the rows of wooden shelves in a soft white glow.

Rory smirked at Melissa. "You're telling me you've never been to the library before?"

"Why would I?" Melissa said. "I don't have time to read. I don't even like when people post long TikTok captions."

"That's because you have a short attention span from all that scrolling," Jillian pointed out as she set off across the creaky, wooden floorboards toward a circulation desk. Behind it a librarian sorted through a stack of books.

"Facts. Scrolling is life." Melissa hurried to catch up. "But if they'd put a little café in here, I would totally swing by. The aesthetic is immaculate."

"Oh! All the drinks could have cute little literary-themed names!" Rory said, getting excited.

"Exactly!" Melissa said. "We could give out bookmarks with the receipts."

"Ooo, yes. Should we do this?" Rory said. "I kinda think wc should."

"You two are always coming up with business ideas,"

Jillian reminded them. All around, books lined the wooden shelves, some with spines so worn they'd lost their color. "And how many of those grand ideas have you actually implemented?"

"Well, none," Melissa said.

"*Yet*," Rory added. "But maybe one day."

Jillian huffed a laugh and stopped at the desk. It was a cherry-brown color and smelled of lemon polish and worn paper. It reminded her of childhood when the au pair would bring her and Shelby to pick out books. Sure, she'd had a bookshelf filled with new purchases in her room, but nothing could beat the feel of coming here and getting to choose her *own* books. The librarian behind the desk had to be at least as old as her mother. She tucked her glasses up into her curly gray hair. "Hello, there," she greeted. "How can I help you?"

"Hi. I called earlier," Jillian said. "We were interested in looking at some of your town records."

"Ah, yes," the woman said. "That's right. You wanted to see our special archives."

Jillian nodded.

"Just follow me." The librarian set off, stepping out from behind the desk to escort them down a hall to a small viewing room filled with metal filing cabinets. There was a large table and chairs in the middle of the room and a white board on the wall. "These cabinets here are where we keep any local historical documents."

Rory tugged on one of the cabinets. "These are locked."

"Some of the records are quite fragile," the woman explained. "We haven't had the chance to have them all digitized yet, so we rarely let visitors into the cabinets on their own." She unlocked one of the cabinets and produced a small box. "When you called earlier and told me what you were looking for, I pulled what I could find on Clyde and Cass Fortune. I'm afraid it wasn't much." She handed Jillian the box. "Feel free to take your time looking at them. We just ask that you be gentle and leave them in the protective plastic coverings."

"Of course," Jillian said. "We'll be very careful." This wasn't her first time working with old documents. She'd even learned how to use a microfiche reader during her short stint as a library assistant in college.

The librarian left them alone, and Jillian sat down at the table. Melissa and Rory crowded in on either side of her. A foolish bloom of excitement stirred in her chest. She didn't know why she was getting her hopes up. She'd found more dead ends than ways forward since starting this search.

"What's that?" Rory asked, pointing down at one of the documents in the box.

"Land titles on the property." Jillian had already seen copies of those in what Nick had helped her get from the county clerk's office. She carefully passed on the plastic-covered document to Rory to have a look, then picked up another piece of paper that announced land for sale out past the railroad tracks. It was an old advert, perhaps from a newspaper clipping, and she wondered if it was this ad that had first drawn Clyde and Cass to purchase their parcel of land. She laid it aside gently for Melissa to look at, but before she could pick up the next document, her phone buzzed.

Jillian pulled it out of her pocket to find a text from Nick. It was a photo of Mandy sitting at a long table with a bunch of other kids, her beaming face smeared in chocolate. Beneath that he wrote, I think the cookies helped some of the kids warm up to her. Who needs to chat when you have chocolate?

Jillian's heart lurched so hard she almost gasped. She didn't realize how hard she was smiling until her cheeks started to ache. Her fingers flew across the keyboard. That's amazing! I told you cookies were a great idea.

You were right.

She replied with a winky face. Keep those words handy, cowboy. You're gonna be using them often.

Nick sent a smirking emoji back. Is that so?

It is.

Well, if you help me figure out how to get her to actually talk to a couple of these kids, I will properly kneel down in front of you, Princess Jillian, ruler of the land of chocolate chips.

Jillian snorted, though she was actually loving every second of this exchange. She was so pleased for Mandy, but even more touched that Nick had reached out to tell her about the success. Seriously, this feels like good progress. Maybe the next step should be show-and-tell day with Otto? Kids love dogs.

That's also a good idea. I'll chat with her teacher. See if we can make that happen.

Are you free for dinner later? Jillian wrote. She was supposed to be meeting Shelby and Cameron to catch up, but why not invite Nick and Mandy along? It was just a casual dinner. Nothing fancy. Does Mandy like pizza?

She loves it.

She texted him the time and place, and Nick sent a thumbs-up. We'll meet you there.

Perfect. She put her phone down before she did something crazy like tack on a heart emoji to her last message.

"What's that smile for?" Melissa said, staring at her with a crooked grin.

"Better yet, *who's* that smile for?" Rory added.

"Just talking to Nick," Jillian said.

"Ooo, Nick," Melissa and Rory said together before breaking into a fit of giggles.

Melissa nudged Jillian. "For real, though. How are things going with the cowboy?"

Jillian bit her lip, trying to contain her smile. "Really good, actually. We've been spending a lot of time together, and we went for a long horseback ride yesterday."

"Please tell me that's a euphemism for—" Rory started to say before Jillian interrupted her.

"A *regular* old horseback ride," she clarified. "Though I might have kissed him a bit."

"Define 'a bit,'" Melissa demanded, clasping her forearm.

Jillian shrugged. "Barely a peck. I didn't want either of us to fall off our horses."

"Jill!" Melissa pretended to faint against the table, making Jillian laugh.

"It's hard to do on horseback, okay? But it's the thought that counts. Or the emotion or whatever. We both obviously wanted to, and that felt nice. After that, we spent the evening at the house making cookies with Mandy. My mother dropped by and got the horrible idea to dig out Shelby's old pageant gowns for the poor kid."

Rory barked a laugh. "You're lucky that didn't scare Nick off. But this is getting kinda serious, huh?"

Jillian sucked in a breath. "I don't know… I don't want to jinx anything before it's official."

"But?" Melissa said.

"*Buuuut...*" Jillian dragged out the word, playing with the edge of the box in front of her. "I kind of think it *is* getting serious. At least on my end. I *really* like him. I didn't expect any of this, especially after our first meeting, but things just feel so easy with Nick. And there's fire there. Beyond just the attraction. So much so that I want to do all the little things with him. Like make dinner and wash dishes and sit on the couch with the dog after Mandy goes to sleep." Her heart raced at the thought. "And I love spending time with Mandy. The world just feels right when we're all together."

"Aww, Jill," Melissa cooed. "Sounds like you've got it bad for the guy. But I'm really happy for you."

"Me too," Rory said. "Nick seems great. He's obviously good with kids—"

"And he's built like a Greek god," Melissa added. "What's not to love?"

Jillian burst into laughter.

"What?" Melissa said, daring them both to argue. "You *know* it's true. I've seen the pictures."

"He is very handsome," Jillian admitted. But truthfully it was his kindness that had won her over, his thoughtfulness, his tenderness. She'd never felt as comfortable with any of the men she'd dated as she did with Nick. For some reason, she felt like all her previous partners had never really understood her, but with Nick, he saw her—even the parts that weren't all that great. The ones she needed to work on. And there was something to be said about a person that saw all your flaws and accepted you anyway. But was that enough? Was it safe to let him and Mandy creep into her heart like this? Despite all the trouble he'd caused, her dad was still in there, occupying a piece of her, and it hurt. If she let Nick get that close, if she let him stay, wouldn't she just be inviting the possibility of more heartache?

"Hey, look at this!" Melissa said suddenly, capturing Jillian's attention. She held up a plastic-covered newspaper article. "It's tiny, only a few lines, but it mentions Clyde and Cass by name."

"What's it say?" Rory asked, leaning against Jillian's shoulder.

Jillian scanned the article. It was incomplete, only part of the paper having survived the years. "The property was being demolished because it had been deemed a hazard by the town council." Melissa handed it over, and Jillian snapped a photo of it. "This must have been sometime after it was foreclosed on."

"You think the property just got run-down with no one living there?" Melissa wondered.

Jillian shrugged, staring at a grainy photo attached to the article. "It's hard to tell from the picture, but the house looks like it's in pretty rough shape." She supposed it was possible that it was like that before the foreclosure. Perhaps Clyde and Cass hadn't been able to afford the upkeep. That was a reasonable conclusion to come to if the property was foreclosed on.

"What now?" Rory wondered.

Jillian texted the photo to the new sibling group chat. It wasn't much to go on other than being the house where Clyde and Cass had once lived. She wanted more though. She was sick of finding incomplete records everywhere they turned. Bits of articles. Missing dates. Redacted information in the lawyers' files. Her father hadn't made this easy on them. She sighed. "Now I see if Hayes's private investigator can dig up any other information."

"That sorta sounds fun," Melissa said. "Ooo, you think Emerald Ridge could use a PI business?"

"Yeah," Jillian joked. "You can set it up right beside your library café."

"Okay, don't hate me," Jillian called as she crossed the parking lot to meet Nick and Mandy as they pulled up outside the restaurant. With twenty different pizzas on the menu, Donatello's Pizzeria was everyone's favorite place for a slice, hands down, no argument. When tourists asked where they should have dinner, Donatello's was always on the list.

Nick narrowed his eyes at her as he stepped out of his truck and closed the driver's door. "What did you do?"

"Nothing to deserve that look," Jillian insisted, tucking her hands into the back pockets of her jeans. "But Shelby and Cameron are coming to dinner."

Nick hummed playfully. "Okay, that's not as bad as I thought."

Jillian laughed. "What were you thinking?"

"That you wanted to change locations to something that was going to require a suit and tie," he admitted.

"I'm wearing jeans," she pointed out.

"Yeah, but you probably keep a classy cocktail dress and heels in your closet for such occasions," he said. "I, on the other hand, think Otto used my one good tie as a chew toy."

"I wouldn't have surprised you like that," she said, laughing at the image of Nick trying to wrestle his clothing away from the dog. She could already tell he was the kind of man who'd be uncomfortable in that kind of fancy setting, and she'd hate to see him not enjoying himself. If they were ever going somewhere that required a dress code, she'd give him plenty of notice. Besides, she knew he'd look good all dressed up, but she was partial to him in his fitted blue jeans. Her stomach flipped, and she had to shove those thoughts aside. "I just wanted everyone to meet."

"I've met your sister," Nick reminded her.

"Yes, but *officially*." Jillian felt her cheeks pink. She didn't know what they were. They hadn't exactly talked about the details, but she didn't usually go around kissing her friends on horseback. So…this was definitely *something.*

"Do they know Mandy's gonna be here?" Nick asked.

Jillian nodded, following him around the truck to Mandy's door. "Of course. Why do you look stressed?"

He shrugged. "I'm not stressed. It's just that not everyone likes to eat with a little kid around."

Jillian's thoughts drifted back to the night Nick had told her about Sylvia. About how she'd left him when she learned that Mandy would be coming to live with him, and her heart broke a little more for him. She reached out and squeezed his hand. "Shelby's about to pop out a kid of her own," Jillian said, trying to lighten the mood. "So she and Cameron could use the practice."

Nick huffed a laugh. "Well, if I'd known that was your goal, I'd have loaded her up on sugar before we got here." He popped the door open, and Mandy smiled back at them, already having half unclipped herself from her car seat.

Jillian double blinked at the girl. "Hello, you. What happened to your hair?"

Mandy touched her pigtails.

"Someone played extra hard at school today and didn't feel like fixing it before the ride over," Nick admitted. He sounded exhausted as he said it.

"Can I help?" Jillian asked.

Mandy nodded.

"Oh, sure," Nick grumbled good-naturedly. "Now you're all cooperative." He helped Mandy hop down from the truck, and she stood perfectly still so Jillian could get her pigtails straightened out.

Jillian was good with kids, she *liked* kids, but with Mandy it felt different. Maternal, almost. She had never thought of herself as mother material, but Mandy made her think differently about things. Something about the little girl tugged at her heartstrings. She worried over the girl and loved to see her smile, and she was so pleased to hear that the cookies went over great with her class. For some reason, it felt important to her to help Mandy feel safe in the world again after losing her parents. And somehow, despite all she'd lost, Mandy seemed to adore Jillian right back. At least enough not to fuss as Jillian fixed her hair.

For a brief moment she imagined doing this in the mornings before Mandy set off for school. She imagined Nick trying to hurry them out the door and her playfully chiding him for rushing them. She imagined untangling Mandy's pigtails at night, running her fingers through the strands. She imagined so hard it hurt. Could she really fit into their world like that? Did Nick want her to?

"There," Jillian said, swallowing down the uncertainty as she twisted Mandy around to face Nick. "Gorgeous! Right, Uncle Nick?"

"Now you're just putting me to shame," he said. "How'd you get them so even?"

Jillian gave him a sly smile. "Trade secrets."

Mandy latched on to her hand and then Nick's, tugging them along toward the divine smell of warm, garlicky bread.

“Someone’s hungry,” Jillian murmured as Mandy reached the large wooden door and attempted to yank it open. Nick gave her a hand, and the child raced inside.

“Oh, this girl can down more pepperoni slices than I can,” Nick said.

Jillian nodded, impressed. “Shelby can probably eat more than both of you combined currently.”

“Well, she can try, but we like pizza, don’t we, Squeaks?” Nick said as they followed her inside.

Mandy nodded, pointing out an empty table.

“We’ve got to wait our turn,” Nick said as they walked up to the hostess’s stand.

“Hi, there,” a waitress said, rushing past. “Someone will be with you in one moment.”

She disappeared, calling over her shoulder to another employee, “Family at the door needs seating.”

Jillian bit back the gasp of surprise that shot up her throat, glancing over at Nick from the corner of her eye. He didn’t seem all that bothered by the assumption they were a family, and her heart skipped a beat. If she was honest, somewhere deep down, she kind of liked the sound of that herself.

But a little voice inside her head questioned if that was a ridiculous dream to have. Nick and Mandy weren’t *hers*. Not yet.

No matter how much she might want them to be.

Chapter Fourteen

Nick stood at the kitchen counter, drying the dinner dishes, his gaze locked on the back of Jillian's head. She was seated on the living room carpet, next to the coffee table, with Mandy cuddled up next to her, so close she was practically hanging off Jillian's neck. His chest clenched at the sight, and he realized he'd been drying the same plate for the past two minutes.

"Oh, this one used to transform into a mermaid!" Jillian announced excitedly as Nick put the plate off to the side. "I wonder if it still works."

"Mermaid?" Mandy parroted.

"It was so cool," Jillian said, digging around in the giant box Agatha had unearthed from storage. It was filled to the brim with Shelby and Jillian's old doll collection. Jillian had brought it over to the cabin earlier that afternoon, wearing a giant grin as she'd dragged it through the door. Then she and Mandy had promptly tore the box apart all over the living room, much to Nick's horror.

There were headless dolls and tiny plastic shoes and itty bitty accessories that he literally needed glasses to see on every surface. Though he supposed there could have been worse things in that box—like pageant dresses.

"I'm confused about the whole transform thing," Nick said. "How does a doll turn into a mermaid?"

"I think it used to have a tail," Jillian replied, smiling at him over her shoulder before digging through the box again. "It was this weird rubbery material, and it actually changed color from pink to purple in warm water."

"Pink!" Mandy said.

Nick pursed his lips. "This feels like highly advanced engineering for a doll." Was Mandy going to start asking for mermaid dolls now instead of stuffed animals at the store?

"Wait until Mandy starts asking you for the dolls that actually go to the bathroom in their fake little diapers," Jillian said.

"You're joking."

"I swear on King's flowing mane."

Nick grimaced. "I'll just take her to the stables if she wants that kind of experience."

Jillian laughed. "Never too early to get her mucking out stalls. Aww..."

"What?" he asked, grinning at the sound.

She looked back at him. "I'm just imagining a Mandy-size pitchfork in the stables."

"Pink?" the child asked again, making them both laugh.

But now Nick was imagining it too—a pint-size, pink pitchfork—and he had to admit it was rather adorable. "I feel like she'd probably be more of a hindrance than a help at this point," he said, lifting his finger and pointing it in Jillian's direction. "So don't get any ideas."

Her smile turned sly. "I promise nothing."

"Jillian—"

"What? If one shows up on your doorstep, it wasn't me."

"She'll probably just use it to jab me in the foot."

Jillian snorted.

"Otto, no!" Mandy cried, drawing Nick's attention as the giant ball of fur tore through the living room, trampling dolls and whipping piles of doll clothes off the coffee table with his tail. He got one of the dolls by the head and went bounding away. Mandy jumped up, chasing him around the dining room table. "*Noooooooo!*"

Jillian slapped her hand over her mouth, clearly trying not to laugh.

"Otto!" Nick said sharply. The dog froze, looked at him, tail wagging—then bounded away, getting the zoomies. He made another round of the living room, launched himself off the recliner and nearly trampled Jillian, who was bent over laughing. Nick abandoned the dishes to carry out a rescue mission, chasing the dog around the living room while Mandy stood there shaking her finger, shouting "Bad doggy!"

"You tell him, Mandy," Jillian encouraged through her laughter.

"Drop it!" Mandy commanded.

At least she is using her words, Nick thought as he snagged Otto by the collar. "Give it here, you little menace."

Otto growled playfully. This wasn't the first toy he'd had to rescue from Otto's slobbery jaws, and he suspected it wouldn't be the last. "This isn't your toy." Nick snagged one of the labradoodle's chew toys from the carpet and offered it up instead. "Here, let's trade."

"Drop it!" Mandy said again, her little brow furrowed.

Otto opened his mouth, and a drool-coated doll rolled free, its head barely attached, hair a tangled mess. Nick released the dog and picked up the doll like it was infected, dangling it over the coffee table. "We might have a casualty," he said. "Think I see a puncture wound."

Mandy pouted, her eyes welling with tears before she threw herself down on the couch.

"*Uncle Nick*," Jillian said, shaking her head at him. "Everything's going to be just fine. We just have to take the doll into surgery." She reached out and patted Mandy's back. "Don't you worry. I've seen cases like this before."

"*Hopeless* cases?" Nick muttered under his breath, grinning as Jillian made a swipe for him. He laughed, handing over the doll.

Jillian was unbothered by the copious amounts of doggy drool, and once again he had a hard time believing this was the same woman he'd once called a princess because of how she'd acted. "We just have to call in the reinforcements."

"Like an undertaker?"

Jillian shot him a look across the coffee table, arching her eyebrow in a way that almost felt flirty. "No, we're breaking out Dr. Dolly. She's a plastic surgeon that specializes in facial reconstruction."

Nick plopped down in the recliner. "Oh, well, that's convenient."

"Isn't it?" Jillian rooted around in the box. "I swear we used to… Wait! I found her little travel medical bag." She popped it open, the bag fitting on her palm. "Ah, yes. Here we are. The necessary supplies. A stethoscope. Tiny Band-Aids." Mandy popped her head up, sliding off of the couch to sit next to Jillian as she pulled out a silver quarter from the bag. "Money. Very handy," Jillian continued.

Nick laughed. "What're you going to do with twenty-five cents?"

"I actually think it was for the payphone," Jillian explained. "That was Shelby's idea."

Nick shook his head. "This surgeon was clearly living through the aughts."

"And loving every minute of it," Jillian said. "Spent her days doing surgery and her nights on the town going to the hottest clubs with her plastic boyfriends."

Nick smirked. "Are these plastic boyfriends in this box?"

"Haven't found them yet. Probably buried at the bottom," Jillian said. "Or maybe Shelby exiled them. She was always having disastrous breakups."

"And you?" he asked. "On the outs with the plastic boyfriends?"

Her lips twisted in amusement. "No, little Jillian wanted to bring a horse to the club."

Nick snorted. "Of course you did."

"I was going to entertain all the dolls with my new one-woman show about winning gold in the equestrian events at the Olympics. It was going to be gritty and filled with drama. But Shelby said the horse and I would have to wait outside because there was no room for a stage and a dance floor in the club." She sighed, shaking her head as if lost in the memory. "There were many falling-outs over dolls. Anyway—" she pressed the tiny stethoscope to the slobbery doll's chest "—I think she's gonna make it, Mandy. Strong heartbeat."

The preschooler picked up the doll, cradling it as she shot Otto a suspicious glare. Thankfully, the dog was now happily chewing on one of his rawhide bones.

"We should try to brush her hair, though," Jillian said. "Can you see if you can find a brush in there?"

Mandy went digging through the box and produced a tiny purple brush. Jillian scraped it through the doll's soggy hair and Nick winced. "I'm surprised more of your dolls aren't bald."

"Oh, trust me. Some of them were." Jillian smirked. "We used to try to glue clumps of their hair back."

"This doll business feels rather dangerous."

"Wait until I find their pink Jeep. Then we'll really get up to some trouble."

"Oh, boy," Nick grumbled. He climbed to his feet to finish putting away the dishes while Jillian continued to chatter to Mandy about the dolls. His niece giggled every now and then, but there wasn't much talking after the Otto incident. Still, even without the words, Nick could tell Mandy had grown quite attached to Jillian, and although that warmed something in his chest, it also made him worry, too. He hadn't forgotten the ache Sylvia had left behind, and he didn't even want to contemplate how they'd both feel if Jillian suddenly stopped showing up to dinner and to the stables and to the cabin with a box of dolls on her hip.

Mandy was falling hard and fast for her, and Nick knew if he wasn't careful, he'd fall under her spell, too. Honestly, he was already halfway there. And still he had no idea what they were—he and Jillian. This woman he spent all his free time with, who he texted every day and shared kisses with on horseback. From where Nick was standing, they'd long stepped over that line of friendship.

She'd introduced him to her sister. Officially. And he'd liked that.

Yet…a small voice called out and told him to hold back. He was moving too quickly. Jillian was the daughter of a billionaire, and he was working two jobs in order to be able to afford to take Mandy to therapy. He couldn't even afford to give his niece the sheer number of dolls Jillian had shown up with today. Their life experiences were completely different, but did that mean they were too different to make a go of it? Nick didn't want to think it would be a problem, but they were living in two different worlds, and he wasn't sure a relationship could survive that. Could Jillian ever truly be happy with him and his simple life? Could she be content with him and Mandy if he didn't have a bank account with an endless number of zeroes? There were people out there who could give her that life. He knew she had options.

And sometimes it was hard to imagine that *he* would be one of her options.

Then again, if all that was true, why was Jillian so easy to talk to? Why was she the first person he wanted to call when something happened with Mandy? And why did she drop by the stables just to see how his day was going? If they were so wrong for each other, why couldn't he stop thinking about holding her, about kissing her? Something had pulled them together, and something *kept* pulling them together. Nick just hoped it was strong enough to bridge the divide between their worlds.

Finally dragging his gaze away from Jillian, he couldn't help wondering if he should be listening to his head…or his heart.

"You know," she was saying to Mandy as he shoved those uneasy thoughts aside. When he glanced back at them, he saw Jillian holding up a doll, pretending it could talk. "Talking to friends is really easy."

Mandy wrinkled her nose and shook her head.

"*It is!*" doll-Jillian insisted. "All you have to do is take a real deep breath." She demonstrated, puffing up her cheeks dramatically, making Mandy laugh. "Then you let it out really quickly." Jillian blew the breath out, rattling her lips together. "If you do it fast enough, the words will come flying out. I promise."

Mandy swallowed a puff of breath, her cheeks inflating.

"There you go," Jillian said. "Now blow it out as fast as you can!"

Mandy sputtered around the breath, making both her and Jillian giggle.

"I don't think it was fast enough," she teased.

Mandy tried it again, puffing up her cheeks, the air leaking out between her lips as she tried to contain her laughter. Nick's chest ached at that sound. *This* was exactly why he wanted to listen to his heart. Because actions were what mattered most, not where a person came from or the kind of family they were born into. Jillian Fortune was the type of person who spent her days with newborns in the NICU and then spent her entire evening baking cookies. She took care of the people she loved, and better yet, she'd chosen to spend her time with them.

Warmth spread through Nick.

"See!" Jillian said. "You keep practicing that, and pretty soon you won't be able to stop talking."

Mandy jumped to her feet and ran over to Nick at the counter. She looked at him with her cheeks puffed up.

"What's that, Squeaks? Can't hear you." He leaned closer, playing along, and when Mandy buzzed her lips together, Nick drew back. "Wow, that was loud!"

Mandy ran away giggling, and Nick caught Jillian's eye, the two of them sharing a long look. Contentment filled him to the brim. He wanted every evening to be like this. He wanted to come home to Jillian Fortune when his work was done, to her smile and her laughter and her warmth, and he wanted *her* to want that, too.

That was the most terrifying thought he'd had in a while.

"Okay," he announced, distracting himself. "Who's ready to brush their teeth?"

Mandy groaned, rolling her eyes at him.

"Last one to the bathroom has to go out and muck the horse stalls," he said.

Mandy gasped and was on her feet, running down the hall before Nick had even made it around the end of the counter.

"Guess you're mucking out the stalls," Jillian quipped as he passed her.

"Guess I am," he said, smiling down at her. "Gonna do the bedtime routine."

"Meanwhile, I'll get this mess contained…" She gestured to the dolls.

Nick lingered in the doorway, watching her for a beat before turning back to get his niece ready for bed. After three stories in a row, Mandy finally passed out, a stuffed animal clutched in each arm. Nick leaned down to kiss her forehead. Then he turned off her lamp and closed the door a smidge before making his way back to the living room. As promised, Jillian had tidied up and carried the box over to the kitchen table. She stood by the dining room window, looking out into the starlit night.

"Heading off?" Nick asked gruffly.

She turned to him and nodded.

He didn't want her to go.

"I've got some more digging to do on Clyde and Cass tomorrow, so I should probably make it an early night."

He *really* didn't want her to go. Not now. Not later. Not tomorrow. And that was a crazy line of thinking. What was he going to do, clear out space in his closet and give her a drawer and ask her if it was enough?

How could it possibly be enough?

"I'll walk you out," he said, following her through the door. The darkness was cozy, the light from the cabin bleeding across the porch, the stars twinkling above. "Thanks for coming by tonight. Mandy had a lot of fun."

"I had a lot of fun with her, too," Jillian said, tucking her arms loosely across her chest.

"Only with her?" Nick teased.

Jillian shrugged. "There might be a cowboy I've grown a little fond of."

Nick couldn't stop the smile that stretched across his face. Whatever his worries were before, they didn't matter now. Because Jillian had infiltrated his heart without even trying. "I've grown fond of you, too."

"I know," Jillian said, her words soft. Warm.

"So, are we only allowed to kiss on horseback now?" Nick asked, his pulse rushing in his ears. His hands itched to reach for her.

Jillian smirked at his question. "I suppose we could try it elsewhere."

"Good," Nick said. "Then get over here." He reached out and took hold of the front of her shirt and tugged her close. Her giggle turned into a gasp as he caught her face between his hands, pressing his lips to hers until all he could feel was fire in his blood. He kissed her the way he'd wanted to kiss her for days, leaving them both breathless at the end of it.

"I'm more than fond of you," Jillian confessed, her words whispered across his cheek.

"I know," he said. Because he was too. "So, are we—"

"Yup," she said, dragging him in for another kiss.

And there, under the stars, that was all Nick needed to know.

Chapter Fifteen

"I told you I have to go," Jillian said, laughing as Nick leaned over the gate of King's pen to kiss her for the… Actually, she'd lost count of how many times.

"Do you?" he teased. "Are you sure?"

"I do. And I am." She'd been trying to leave the stables for the last half hour, but every time she brought up leaving, Nick would cock his head and arch his eyebrow beneath his Stetson, and butterflies would erupt in her belly.

How she'd ever gone a day without thinking that Nick Slater was the most handsome man in the world, she didn't know. Trailing him around during chore time had become her new favorite pastime, especially when it meant indulging in her other favorite thing: the horses. It had been weeks since she'd felt the tight unease in her chest walking into these stables. The space had quickly become synonymous with Nick in a way that ate away at the uncertainty surrounding her dad's death.

"Those babies are lucky to have you," he said.

"I don't know about that." Jillian protested. "The nurses are probably most appreciative. Too many babies and not enough time to show them all the necessary loving."

He tilted his head, his eyes flashing with something

wicked. She could almost hear what he wasn't saying. *I'd like to show you some necessary loving.*

Or maybe that was just what *she* wished he would say. She'd been picturing Nick in her bed a lot recently, and she wasn't quite sure how to stop it. Frankly, she didn't *want* to. Her craving for him deepened with each passing day. She longed to know the feel of his skin against hers, the sound of his voice rumbling in the dark. She imagined the sheets whispering over them as they twisted against each other. More than anything, she ached to discover all the ways Nick could make her feel good.

Because somehow they'd found each other in this mess, and it seemed to be working. The way he looked at her, his blue eyes twinkling, she wanted to believe they'd found something good, and Jillian was so excited to be able to build something great together—a little life with Nick and Mandy. Her heart raced as she thought it. She'd never wanted anything more. But they're not yours, the voice in her head whispered. *Not really.*

Nick and Mandy had a sweet little life together, and Jillian wanted to be part of that. She wanted to belong. But could she when her life was still filled to the brim with Archibald's drama? And if their worlds didn't align perfectly, could she risk getting even more attached? Opening her heart wouldn't just leave room for her to be disappointed. Losing Nick and Mandy now would be devastating, and that thought momentarily flared like the pain of grief in her chest.

"What time will you be home?" Nick asked.

"Not until later tonight," she told him. "I'm meeting Madeline after my shift to chat through theories on Clyde and Cass." She should also really check in with Hayes to see how he was doing with the Penn situation.

"Well, can I maybe interest you in a post-dinner drink?" he murmured. "Once you're back and Mandy has gone to bed? You can drop by and tell me all about your day."

That sounded lovely. "I'd like that," she said, wondering when the butterflies in her gut were going to give it a rest. "You're sure it won't be too late?"

"I think I can wait up for you."

"You're *really* sure?" she said seriously. She didn't want to keep him up late when she knew how busy his days were.

He shrugged playfully. "Yeah, you're worth it."

Jillian's lips twisted into a smile. "All right then, cowboy. I'll bring you some dessert or something."

"Now these are the perks I'm here for."

"Mm-hmm," she said. "I'm sure they are."

King huffed, nuzzling at Nick's back, getting impatient. "I should get back to work before this guy gives me a swift kick."

"He wouldn't do that," Jillian cooed, reaching up to pat King's forelock. "He's the best boy."

Nick leaned over the gate once more and kissed her cheek. "Have fun snuggling babies."

"I always do."

Forty-five minutes later, Jillian had parked, made her way up to the NICU, chatted with the nurses and settled herself into a recliner chair for a cuddle session with a tiny bundle asleep on her chest.

"Aren't you just the cutest?" she whispered down to the little boy, her hands gently holding him in place. The baby was warm against her skin, his weight hardly noticeable, and her heart skipped at how precious he was. "You're looking strong. I bet you'll get to go home soon," she said softly, wondering if the baby could feel the soft vibration of her words. "And I bet your family can't wait for that moment." Her thoughts drifted to Shelby and her soon-to-be nephew. "They've probably got the nursery all set up for you."

Jillian knew that finally getting to bring this little bundle home would make all these seemingly endless, scary weeks worth it. She'd been volunteering here long enough to have seen those moments herself, and they always warmed her heart and brought tears to her eyes. But part of her wished she could do more for these children, for these families, for all the kids that spent time in the hospital. She wished she could bring them slivers of joy even when they were stuck in here enduring the tests and the procedures.

If only there was a way to make these hard things a little easier.

Jillian heard a familiar laugh, her eyes lifting to the nurses' station that was visible through the sliding glass doorway that separated the NICU from the hall. She spotted Sam Cartwright, the director of the children's department, leaning up against the desk, chatting with the nurses. He was gray-haired and rarely serious, except when it came to his job. Sam had a soft heart and a joke for anyone that needed one. He ran in similar circles to her dad—or the ones her dad *had* run in. Jillian had met him a fair few times around the hospital or at gala events over the years.

"Ms. Fortune," he said as the sliding glass doors parted to allow him entry.

She rolled her eyes, giving him a gentle smile. "Hi, Sam. You know you can call me Jillian, right?"

"Jillian," he said, giving her a wink. "I see I'm not the only one who likes to pop in for my daily dose of serotonin."

"They really are great for that. How can anything bother you when you're surrounded by this much cuteness?" She grinned as the baby on her chest stirred. "I mostly like to sit in here with them and imagine these babies twenty years from now, happy and thriving."

"The things they might do," Sam said in agreement. He arched a bushy eyebrow. "The people they might become."

"Maybe they'll be doctors that work in this very hospital," Jillian added, imagining it. "Or nurses. Or volunteers."

"Or maybe they'll be the kind of people that donate to make sure our children are provided with the most comprehensive care for years to come."

Jillian frowned a bit at his words, her hand rubbing a gentle circle against the baby's back. She wasn't quite sure what Sam was referring to.

"You know what I learned today?" he said, a strange note in his voice

She shook her head. "What?"

"That your father made a sizable donation to the children's department in your name." Sam peered into one of the incubators being used to keep another little baby warm. "It was one of the terms of his will."

Jillian blinked at him, stunned. "I—I had no idea."

"Neither did I," Sam admitted. "He was always very generous during our yearly fundraisers. But this donation..." He whistled. "It's going to allow us to do a lot of good, Jillian. You should be very proud."

Jillian frowned even more. She was grateful for her dad's donation, of course—thankful that it would provide such good care for the children of Emerald Ridge. But the way the director said it... She felt like she was missing something. Why had the donation been made in *her* name? It didn't make sense, especially considering how many strings Archibald had put on her receiving her portion of the inheritance. What did she have to do with how her dad spent his money?

Sam must have understood her confusion because he walked over and placed a hand on her shoulder. For a beat he reminded her of her father. It was the charcoal suit and the way he wore his hair swept back, the once dark locks now streaked white and gray. He even smelled like Dad had—aftershave and espresso. Her chest clenched. "He made the donation because he was so proud of your volunteering efforts here, Jillian. Did you know Archibald used to visit the hospital himself from time to time?"

Jillian shook her head, feeling an unwanted weight behind her eyes. "I didn't."

"He'd stop by my office on occasion, and we'd walk together, and he'd tell me that he could have used volunteers as wonderful as you when he was younger."

Jillian's throat grew thick. Volunteers for what? She swallowed convulsively, barely able to force the words out. "Oh, that's—"

"I know things must be...difficult right now," Sam continued, letting his hand drift from her shoulder. "I won't pretend I haven't heard the rumors, but whatever complicated past your father left behind, he also left a lot of good behind in this world, too. Good that he believed in. And that includes you, Jillian. So, for what it's worth, I'm sorry he's gone."

"Thanks, Sam," she said, feeling like she was scrapping the words off the roof of her mouth. "That means a lot."

"I'll let you get back to it. Babies are more fun than listening to the ramblings of an old man anyway."

Jillian held down a surge of feelings as the gentleman walked away—confusion and anger...longing and despair—feeling heat burn through her insides. She watched Sam disappear through the sliding glass door and drift down the hall. Jillian clamped her mouth shut. It felt like if she opened it, a horrible sound might escape. It was only the tiny weight next to her heart that kept her grounded.

What was she supposed to think after that? She was touched by her dad's donation. Who wouldn't be? But if the donation was a term of his will, that meant it was something he'd *really* thought about, something he'd cared enough about to pre-plan. Sam's words echoed in her head.

He left a lot of good behind in this world.

Hearing that her dad had been proud of her volunteering… Jillian had never felt all that close to him, but right now, in this moment with that tiny baby on her chest, she wished it was different. She wished she'd understood her dad and his childhood and how he'd become Archibald Fortune—billionaire, business mogul, father of six. She never thought he wanted to know her, but this donation proved that maybe he did. Maybe he'd believed she had potential. And if they'd had a better relationship, they could have talked about that. Frustration flared in her chest, because he'd thrown money at a cause she was passionate about, and she was only now finding out.

If he'd told her, they might have bonded. But he hadn't given her that chance.

Jillian released a sharp breath. She was conflicted. The donation was incredible, but the intent felt almost manipulative. Was this once again her father trying to push her in a direction he approved of, the way he'd once pushed her away from acting?

No, she told herself. *That doesn't matter.*

She was old enough to make her own decisions, and she already knew she wanted to do more for these children, not just financially the way her dad had.

She wanted to be a real presence for these kids. But how? How did she spark joy in a place that was so often big and scary and full of the unfamiliar?

Her thoughts strayed to Mandy and the way her face lit up every time Nick called Jillian a princess. *Hmm...* she thought, an idea swirling around her mind. Perhaps there was something there. Perhaps there was a way to bring these children a little bit of joy using the things they already loved. Something that would make them feel safe and secure and brave in the face of uncertainty.

Were those the things her dad had been missing in his childhood—joy, safety, security? She wanted to know now more than ever, but her dad was long gone and, sadly, so were those answers.

Chapter Sixteen

By the time Jillian made her way back to the ranch that night, she was mentally exhausted. Volunteering at the hospital, which usually brought her such joy, had left her questioning *so* many things. Still, she hadn't wanted her heavy thoughts to dampen her afternoon with Madeline. She'd realized that all the siblings had each had different relationships with their dad, and the last thing Jillian wanted was to spoil her half sister's memories more than they already were. So she'd held on to her unease all day, turning her focus back to the Clyde and Cass mystery. But now things had been stewing in her mind for so long she felt the burden of them press down on her like a physical weight.

Plus, if she was being honest, there was really only one person she wanted to talk to right now, and as she made her way up the porch steps to Nick's cabin, he stood leaning against the open doorway in his fitted blue jeans and a snug gray shirt, waiting to greet her.

"Well, what a surprise," he joked, his voice rough and yet soft. He gave her a crooked little smile. For some stupid reason, she almost burst into tears at the sight. Jillian blinked away the feeling, got a hold of herself, then crossed the porch almost at a run, sinking into his arms. "Hey," he said.

"Hi," she croaked.

He pressed his lips to the top of her head, nuzzling against her hair as he inhaled. "Long day?" he asked when she sighed.

"Yeah," she admitted. *Long. Confusing. Upsetting.*

"C'mon," Nick said, taking her by the hand and tugging her into the cabin. "I'll get you a drink, and you can tell me all about it."

Jillian let him lead her to the couch, sinking down onto one of the cushions. She accidentally sat on a stuffed bear, but she wasn't sure if it was Mandy's or Otto's. Judging by how quiet it was, she assumed the little girl was already in bed. Otto was splayed out on the floor, his tail flicking occasionally, probably caught up in some dream where he got to chase horses around the ranch.

"Beer?" Nick asked, heading for the fridge.

"Sure," she said.

He brought two over, sitting down on the couch beside her. She leaned against him, the heat of his body leaching into hers, and she thought about how nice it was. The first time they'd sat on this couch together, the first time he'd kissed her, she'd been so nervous. And now… Well, it felt right. Being here with him felt like what she was supposed to do.

What she *wanted* to do.

Her pulse raced as he tucked his arm around her. They hadn't moved past the kissing stage yet—they were both so busy, and there was Mandy to think about, and well, she hadn't wanted to *rush* it. But as he held her close and ran his fingertips up and down her bare arm, she thought about how much she wanted him.

"Everything go okay with the NICU babies?" he murmured.

Jillian hummed. "They were very well behaved today."

"Yeah, I imagine they can cause a real ruckus when they get going," Nick joked.

Jillian laughed softly. "I did have a conversation with Sam Cartwright. He's the director of the—"

"Children's department," Nick said, nodding. "I've met him a few times while at Mandy's therapy appointments."

"He used to run in the same local circles as my dad," Jillian explained.

"Oh yeah?" Nick said, laying his other hand on her knee. "How was that?"

Jillian watched him rub small circles against her leg and fought off the delicious shiver that crawled up her spine. "Well, he told me that my dad left a sizable donation to the children's department in my name as part of his will."

"I…" Nick squeezed her a little. "Jillian, that's amazing."

Her throat grew thick. "It really is. They're going to be able to help a lot of children get the care they need."

"You didn't know?"

She shook her head. "That's not the kind of thing that Dad and I ever would have discussed." Frankly, they didn't talk about the *usual* things. Why would they have discussed his will?

"That's an incredible donation. And in *your* name." He kissed her temple. "You obviously inspire a lot of people."

"Do I?"

"You inspire me."

She turned to look at him, seeing nothing but sincerity in his eyes. "Sam said my dad talked about how proud he was of me." Her throat grew tighter, her chest aching, her eyes welling with tears. She swiped at them. "I'm sorry. I don't know why I'm so upset about this."

Nick caught her face with his hand, cradling her cheek.

"Hey..." He pressed his forehead to hers for a beat, then pulled back. "It's okay. You're allowed to be upset."

Jillian nodded. "I think I'm still a little stunned. I didn't even realize that he paid attention to the fact that I volunteered there. And then it turns out he did. He *noticed* me. Noticed how much volunteering with the children meant to me." Her chin wobbled as she spoke. "I spent my whole life wanting that. Wanting him to notice me, to pay attention to me, to spend more time with me. And it just sucks, you know? To realize only after he was gone that we maybe could have bonded over these things."

"I'm sorry it's been so hard, darlin'" Nick said. His thumb brushed at a tear. Jillian managed to blink most of them away.

She sighed. "My dad and I could never figure things out, and I thought I'd made my peace with that. Thought I was okay with not really having him in my life. But now that he's gone, I regret not trying harder."

"I think he also needed to try harder," Nick said. "From everything you've told me."

"You're right," Jillian agreed thickly. "I'm not letting him off the hook for that, or for keeping everything a secret for so long, but I wish I'd made an effort to know more about him while I still had the time."

"That's the hard thing," he said. "I think we'd all make more of an effort if we knew we were going to be robbed of the years we'd always imagined. I was angry at my brother for a while, for leaving way before it was his time, but I was also ticked at myself for not making more of an effort." He took a breath and rubbed the back of his neck. "When Mandy came along, they just got so busy, and I wanted to leave them alone to live their lives. I still saw him, still spoke to him, but the weekly calls turned to monthly, and the visits became holidays and special occasions. I think life throws a lot at us, and that comes with regrets."

"Sure does," she concurred. "Shelby's better at hiding it, but Dad hurt us a lot over the years by not showing up, not being around. So I guess I'm a little annoyed at myself for feeling this way in the first place. I never thought I'd be sitting here wishing I could go back and do things differently, because *he* was the one who chose to hold us at a distance. But now I'm also wondering how many times he might have tried to offer an olive branch that I didn't bother seeing." Her voice grew strained again, and Nick smiled at her softly. "He's gone and done this amazing thing for the hospital, and I can't even thank him for it."

"I'm sure he knew how grateful you'd be."

"I don't know," Jillian muttered. "I was so hard on him growing up. Back then it felt like he didn't care enough to make time for me or Shelby or Mama, and even though I know why now, it doesn't make any of that hurt less."

"I'm not sure anything will make that hurt less," Nick admitted.

Jillian nodded. Her dad's rejection still burned in her chest after all these years, and part of her wondered if she now walked through life trying to protect herself from similar rejection. She lived in this privileged reality, the world at her fingertips, but truthfully, the circle of people she really trusted was quite small. She thought about the day she'd met Nick and Mandy, about how she hadn't noticed them around before—something she still felt terrible about—but maybe that was the way she was with a lot of people. If she didn't notice them, if she didn't give them the opportunity to get close to her, then they couldn't disappoint her.

But the truth was, Nick and Mandy had already slid past her defenses, and the last thing she wanted was to be rejected again. To be told there was no space for her in their lives. She didn't think she could handle that. Jillian swallowed hard, burying that fear. "Sometimes it feels like I'm stuck between loving him and hating him."

"Maybe that's okay," Nick said, his shoulder lifting in a shrug. "Maybe you don't have to pick one or the other. You can love him and hate him and miss him and wish things could be different. You can have all those feelings at once, just like different versions of your father existed at once. He can be the amazing man that made that donation in your name and still be the shitty, absentee father."

Jillian blinked at him. She'd been trying so hard to reconcile the man she'd learned he was with the man she thought he was, that she'd never stopped to consider that she didn't have to. She could simply accept that her dad was imperfect, and though she *did* love him, she didn't have to be okay with the person he was to her. "I'd never thought of it that way."

"Humans are complicated. I think if you work on accepting that your father was one of those complex individuals, you'll feel less pressure to forgive him simply because he's gone."

"Does that make me a horrible person?" she asked quietly.

Nick tucked his finger under her chin and lifted it. "You're one of the best people I've ever known—and more people deserve to get to know you, Jillian. To be close to you."

His words were whispered across her face. She reached her palm up toward his cheek and kissed him. *Really* kissed him.

"Thank you for listening," she said, pulling back slightly.

"Of course," he rasped, his words warm against her lips. "Always."

Her chest tightened at that. Did he mean that the way she thought he meant that? Would he really always be there for her like this?

Jillian licked her lips, looking into those blue, *blue* eyes. God, she wanted him. She tugged at his collar, pulling him down to the couch cushions with her, their lips fused as heat burned between them.

"Wait!" he husked.

She frowned as he pulled back. "What?" Did he not want this? Oh, no. She groaned internally. Had she read the entire moment wrong? "You don't—"

"Oh, I do," Nick assured her quickly. "More than anything."

That settled her immediate nerves.

"But not with Otto watching."

A laugh got caught in her throat as she turned to face the pup that was still flopped on the floor, his tail wagging uncontrollably now that Nick had said his name. "You're kidding, right?"

"I don't want him judging me," Nick said, climbing to his feet. He reached for her, pulling Jillian up so quickly her head spun and she toppled into his arms. He dipped her briefly. "Well, hello, princess. Care to see the royal bedchambers?"

She snorted. "You're never gonna let this princess thing go, are you?"

"Hell no," he answered, then he righted them, lacing their fingers together as he led her from the living room. "Mind your business," he jokingly said to Otto as they passed. The furball gave his tail a wag and yawned.

Nick led her down the hall, pausing once to kiss her in

the dark. It ignited sparks in her again, and Jillian whimpered, the sounds swallowed up as Nick deepened the kiss, tongue parting her lips to taste the inside of her mouth.

Jillian would have melted to the floor if not for his strong arms holding her up.

He kissed her lips again, then her jaw and neck, cradling the back of her head as sensation shot through her, pooling in her belly. His touch was divine, and she gasped as his fingers slipped beneath her shirt, carving paths along her waist to her lower back with his calloused hands. Jillian had never wanted anything more than she wanted to be in Nick's arms right now.

As Nick pulled back, breaking the kiss, Jillian sucked in a shaky breath. He smiled at her in that dim hallway, reaching for a lock of her hair. He twirled it between his fingers. "You're sure?" he asked, his voice low and rough.

"Yes," she said. "Are you?"

"I've wanted to do this for weeks," he admitted, the corner of his mouth curving.

"Then why didn't we?"

"I guess… I wanted to make sure it was real… You know, I didn't want to be bringing people in and out of Mandy's life."

She nodded and threaded her hand through his again. "I get that and just so you know, this is real for me." She hoped he could tell she was serious. She thought he could, with the way he was looking at her. She curled her free hand in the fabric of his shirt and hauled him close enough to kiss again. "So, about these royal bedchambers?"

Nick grinned and surprised her by sweeping her off her feet and into his arms, carrying her down the rest of the hall. She giggled against him, her arms ringed around his neck, trying not to wake Mandy. "Is this the princess treatment?" she murmured.

"It's everything you deserve," he said thickly. Her heart thumped as he carried her into his room, kicking the door closed behind him. He deposited her onto his bed. She tried to get her bearings in the dark, tried to define the shadows in his room. Bedpost, Stetson on a tall dresser, a mirror. But all she really cared about was his weight against hers, pushing her back into the bed. She kissed him and Nick deepened it, his tongue seeking entrance. Jillian parted her lips and let herself float away with the desire coursing through her veins. Her heart was hammering so hard, when he laid his palm against her chest, he must have been able to feel it.

For several long minutes, there was nothing but the sound of them rustling out of their clothes and heavy panting breaths as Nick touched her. He stroked her *everywhere*, and Jillian never wanted it to end. She wanted him so damn bad she could hardly bear the ache between her thighs.

"You're—"

"I'm sure," she said again. Jillian was also sure she was going to explode if he didn't do something soon. She felt him shift, heard the squeak of a drawer next to the bed and the crinkle of a wrapper.

She ran her hands along his shoulders as he fumbled with the condom, her palms running over every glorious, muscled inch of his chest. "Where're you going, cowboy?" she asked, laughing a bit as he wriggled down her body, leaving a trail of kisses against her stomach.

"Just doing what I do best," he said. "Caretaking the land…checking over the terrain." He teased her with a kiss to her thigh.

A gasp launched up her throat.

"You like that?" he asked, pressing a kiss to her other thigh.

"Yes," she sighed into the darkness, parting her legs as he settled against the place she wanted him most. And then he ravished her with lips and tongue, and Jillian moaned.

"Keep it down, princess," Nick whispered against her skin, sending electric shivers through her. He got back to work, and her vision blanked to nothing but stars as he unraveled her, leaving her trembling and moaning his name.

When he climbed back up her body, the scruff of his jaw tickled against her cheek. Jillian felt him inhale, sensed the question on his tongue, but she wanted it. She was ready. And she curled her leg over his hip to tell him as much. Nick pressed up on his forearms, looking down at her. She nodded her head and braced her hands on his shoulders as Nick sank slowly against her. The stars returned and she writhed beneath him as she came undone again, as he showed her what it really was to be taken care of.

When it was over, they lay there in the soft aftermath, warm and content, wrapped up in each other. Nick's breathing grew even and deep, and Jillian sighed, a smile on her lips, feeling seen, feeling cared for, feeling safe for the first time since her family had stumbled into this mess. She ran her hand along his big, broad shoulder. She worried sometimes that their lives were so different, but there were no doubts in her mind now how perfectly they fit together. Sure, they had their differences, but where it really mattered, they *connected*. And it might just be all the delicious endorphins still coursing through her, but for the first time in a long time, things felt like they were going to be okay.

Chapter Seventeen

Mandy was in a mood.

Nick had forgotten that she didn't have school today, and apparently the fact that he'd forgotten to tell *her* that had been the most grievous of crimes. She'd walked out of her room this morning, in a sundress and mismatched socks, and he'd had to break the news.

She'd wanted to show off her new dress today—the one dotted with sunflowers that Jillian had helped them pick out on a recent shopping trip. And when he'd told her otherwise, she'd promptly stomped her foot at him and thrown herself down face first on the couch.

Can't exactly blame her, he thought as he yawned. It wasn't like he had the energy for morning chores himself—not when he was this tired. He and Jillian had been seeing a lot of each other these past few days, and they'd been having a very, *very* good time. Nick was still a little surprised at how easily they'd come together, how perfect it felt, as if she was a piece he'd been missing all along. It was almost funny to see how far they'd come in such a short time, from misjudging her that day in the stables to wanting to spend every moment with her. The woman he'd gotten to know over these past weeks was sweet and kind and caring. And sure, maybe he still felt a little behind at times, trying to keep up with the world she belonged to, but at the end of the day, Jillian was there, waiting for him with a smile. Waiting for him *and* Mandy.

She didn't care that he wasn't some trust-fund guy.

Or that he lived in this tiny cabin or drove a beat-up truck or spent his days getting dusty in the stables.

She'd proven that again and again.

Mandy poked her head up from the couch, her blond hair a mess as she looked at him.

"Got it out of your system?" he asked her. She rolled her eyes so dramatically Nick laughed. "It's too early for that kind of sass, young lady. You can wear your sunflower dress to school on Monday, okay?"

Mandy looked at the fridge, narrowing her eyes.

Nick walked over to check the calendar posted there. "I'm double checking right now. Yep, you got school Monday." He sighed. With no school and no sitter arranged, he didn't have much other choice. He'd have to bring her along to the stables. "Why don't you go change so you don't get your dress all dirty, huh?"

Mandy pursed her lips at him.

"C'mon, Squeaks. It'll be fun. I'll let you bring some apple slices to feed the horses." That seemed to catch her attention because she climbed off the couch and ran down the hall to her room.

By the time Nick had cut up the apples, wrangled Mandy into a pair of overalls suitable for the stables and actually got to work, they were a little late. And once she was finally done petting all the horses and offering up her apple slices, he was really behind.

"All right, you sit here," he said, parking her on a stool. After setting her up with an episode of her favorite TV program on his phone, he began to muck out a nearby stall.

He'd only turned around for two minutes, rushing through the job, but when he looked back, she'd disappeared.

"Mandy?" he called, whipping his head left and right as he scanned the stables. He spotted her running down the aisle toward a large stack of hay bales. Nick sighed. This was obviously what people meant when they said kids thrive on routine. Right now, neither of them was thriving. "Mandy?" he called, his tone serious. "Get your behind back here."

She stopped in her tracks, then turned around and slumped back in his direction. He knew she wanted to play, but the stables weren't the best place for that, especially when she was unsupervised.

"You can't be on the hay bales, okay?" he said, getting her settled on the stool again. "They could tumble. You could fall. I know they look like fun, but they're off-limits. Got it?"

She nodded.

He narrowed his eyes, pressing his forehead to hers. "You sure you got it, missy?"

She laughed a bit. He put on a different show on his phone, this one with talking dogs, and went back to work. It continued on like that for another half hour. He started working, Mandy got bored and went wandering, and Nick had to chase her back within sight.

"Amanda Slater!" he called as she went running down the aisle again. "Don't make me come get you!"

"Looks like you could use some backup," Jillian joked, walking toward him.

"*Mandy!*" he shouted again as she started climbing one of the gates to peer in at the horses. He trusted the animals, but the last thing he needed was for her to get nipped because she stuck her little fingers where they didn't belong.

"No school?" Jillian asked.

"No, not today." Nick shot her a grin. Just the sight of Jillian stirred contentment in his chest. Well, contentment and something *else*. He let his gaze drift for a second, taking in every inch of the gorgeous woman in front of him before getting back to business. "I forgot or else I'd have asked Des to cover this morning or found a sitter or something."

Mandy climbed down from the gate and went skipping to the next one, holding her hand out to try to call the horse over. Nick sighed.

"I've got her," Jillian said. "You keep doing sexy cowboy things."

Nick smirked. "Mucking the stalls turns you on, does it?"

She flicked the brim of his Stetson then turned her head to peck him on the cheek. "I'll show you just how much later."

Jillian set off after Mandy, the girl squealing as Jillian caught her under the arms and lifted her off the gate. The sound of his niece's laughter warmed something in Nick, and if he took an extra moment to appreciate Jillian's backside as she walked away… Well, who could blame him?

Nick picked up his pitchfork again and finished cleaning the stall. Then he turned King out to the pasture so he could make quick work of his stall, too. After that, Nick fed and watered some of the other horses and organized the tack room. He could hear Mandy giggling all the way across the stables. Picking up a brush, he went to see one of the Andalusian horses when a sharp cry caught his attention.

He perked his head up, one hand still pressed to the glossy gray coat in front of him, and once again heard a wail carry across the stables. *Mandy.*

Nick dropped the brush and raced out of the stall. “Mandy?” he called.

“We’re over here!” Jillian replied.

He followed Jillian’s voice and the sound of Mandy’s cries. His entire body ran cold. He’d learned the difference between a cry for attention and a tantrum and a genuine cry of pain over the last year. And *that* was a cry of pain. He spotted Jillian hunched over by the stack of hay bales that he’d told Mandy not to mess around with earlier and jogged over.

“What happened?” Nick demanded, breathless as he reached them.

Jillian was crouched on the ground next to Mandy, whose face was streaked with tears. She squeezed her right arm to her chest.

“She was just playing,” Jillian explained. “And she fell.”

“Off the *hay bales*?” he bit out, frustration and fear surging through him in equal measure. “I told her she wasn’t supposed to be on the hay bales. She *knew* that.” He was pretty sure Jillian should have known better, too. This wasn’t a playground.

Mandy’s sobs started up again as she looked at him with those glassy blue eyes. For a flash of a second, he saw his brother and his insides twisted painfully.

“Oh, Shelby and I used to climb the hay bales all the time,” Jillian was saying. “We sometimes got a little bumped and bruised.” Her voice was soft and calm. It made Nick’s blood boil. She ran her hand over Mandy’s head. “It’ll be all right, sweetheart.”

Does this damn well look all right? Nick wanted to snap. His hands trembled and his heart pounded against his ribs.

“Can I see?” Jillian asked Mandy, gesturing to her arm.

The little girl shook her head, squeezing her eyes tight. "Hurts," she blubbered, crying harder. "Hurts!"

Big fat tears welled in her eyes, and Nick's stomach sank. This was no bump or bruise. She was seriously injured. His pulse skipped a beat, then he shoved that sickening surge of fear aside, scooped Mandy into his arms and raced for his truck.

Nick had no idea how the hell he'd gotten to the hospital. Everything between the ranch and pediatric unit had been a blur of adrenaline and tears and Jillian's too-calm words as she talked to Mandy through the drive. Nick hadn't even stopped to pay the parking meter as he rushed Mandy into urgent care.

They'd done an intake with Mandy blubbering in his arms, refusing to let the nurses touch her arm, and the next thing he knew she was in a tiny hospital gown, wailing as some guy that looked too young to be an actual doctor poked and prodded at her. Then he had to listen to her sob as she was wheeled off for X-rays into a room where he couldn't accompany her.

"It'll be okay," Jillian said to him, running her hand up and down his arm. "X-rays are quick, and then she'll be right back."

Nothing about this was okay! Nick stiffened at her touch, anger coiling his every nerve, and he felt about thirty seconds from having a complete breakdown himself.

Mandy was crying silent tears when she was finally returned to the small corner of the ward that they occupied. She practically leapt out of the wheelchair at him when the porter pulled up next to the bed. Jillian was talking again, but Nick had no idea what she was saying. He couldn't hear past the rush of blood in his ears. In fact, he couldn't hear anything until the doctor returned with a smile on his face and announced, "Looks like a sprain."

Just a sprain.

Not broken.

Nick couldn't even begin to relax. The doctor offered Mandy a sticker. She sniffled and accepted it.

"You're going to want to follow RICE for the next forty-eight hours or so," the doctor said. "Rest, ice, compression, elevation."

Nick nodded. He'd been in enough tumbles over the years to know that.

"I'm going to get one of the nurses to stop by and put Mandy's arm in a splint," the doctor continued, "just to give her wrist some added support, and to teach you how to tie a sling. If she's uncomfortable, you can try some over-the-counter pain medication."

"Thanks, Doc," Nick said, his heart still racing. He looked down at Mandy, knowing things could have been so much worse. He never should have taken his eyes off her. Or trusted her with anyone but himself. The doctor clapped Nick on the shoulder. "Nurse should be in shortly, then you folks are good to go."

Nick plopped Mandy down on the bed carefully and stepped beyond the curtain for a breather. The ward hummed with machines and the tread of footsteps. He heard Jillian offer to help Mandy put her sticker on her hospital gown, then Jillian joined him outside.

"Looks like she might nod off," Jillian said. "Poor thing probably exhausted herself from crying so hard."

Nick dropped his head into his hands, rubbing at his eyes. His whole body was thrumming in a way he hated. It felt like he'd stuck his finger in an electrical socket.

"Hey," Jillian said, touching his shoulder. Her tone was

soft, soothing, and part of him wanted to tip into her embrace, but he couldn't. He was still too tightly wound. "It's okay," she said. "Everything's *okay*. Kids are always getting hurt. It's not a big deal. They bounce back really quickly."

"Not a big deal?" he growled, dropping his hands. How was she so nonchalant about Mandy's injury? Had she not heard Mandy's sobs? Or watched her squirm as the doctor twisted her arm back and forth? "How can you even *say* that?"

Jillian's eyes widened at his tone. "I just meant—"

"I heard what you said." He gestured in Mandy's direction. "You were supposed to be watching her."

"I *was* watching her," she told him.

"Well, obviously not close enough. She never should have been climbing the hay bales. You should have known better."

Jillian crossed her arms. "Kids do silly things, Nick. They play, they fall down. They scuff their knees. Then they get back up and do it all over again. That's part of being a kid. Part of growing up."

"This is part of being a kid?" he snapped. "Hospital visits. Wrist sprains?"

"Sometimes," Jillian said, hushing him. "Not so loud. You're going to scare her."

Nick sneered and shook his head. "You don't get it."

Her eyes narrowed. "What don't I get exactly?"

He lowered his voice but couldn't stop it from shaking. "Mandy is all I have left of my brother, and I need to be there for her."

"You are there for her," Jillian insisted.

Nick clenched his jaw. He couldn't do this with Jillian. Not anymore. He needed to focus on Mandy and her needs, not dilute his attention when he already had to work so hard to provide for her. And Jillian… God, he cared about her, but she was a distraction. And if he was distracted, he wasn't being a good uncle. He couldn't be the reason Mandy continued to get hurt.

"Talk to me," she urged. "What are you thinking?"

"I can't do this," Nick said as the realization hit him. It was like getting kicked in the chest by a horse. He needed to let Jillian go. For his sake. For Mandy's.

"I don't… What are you saying?" Jillian asked, her brow furrowing. "I don't understand."

"This…*us*. I'm sorry," Nick said, gesturing between them. His insides felt like they'd been boiled. "I just… Mandy needs more from me. She needs to be my sole focus."

"Nick, look," Jillian said, her tone pleading. "I know you were worried today, but she's going to be—"

"No." He shook his head sharply. "I can't be with you anymore, Jillian." As far as he was concerned, they were over. He *needed* this to be over.

Jillian's mouth hung open, the shock written into her beautiful features in a way that made Nick regret every word. But he couldn't… Mandy had to be everything.

"You're serious?"

"I am."

Jillian nodded slowly, looking away from him, her eyes glassy. Nick felt wretched inside. "Tell Mandy I hope she feels better," she whispered. And then she turned on her heel and walked right out of his life.

Chapter Eighteen

"You wanna talk about it yet?" Shelby asked, standing in the doorway of Jillian's bedroom.

"Talk about what?" Jillian said as she danced back and forth in front of the mirror, running her hands down the front of her blouse. She was meeting Melissa and Rory downtown in an hour, and nothing she put on felt right. Nothing she *did* felt right. It had been that way for days now.

Her sister sighed dramatically and crossed her arms over her baby bump. "Mama said you've been avoiding the stables."

"So?" Jillian said, turning away from the mirror and heading back into her closet. She stripped out of the blouse and tried on a new one. Immediately, she regretted it. It was the same shirt she'd been wearing the day she went to meet Nick for the first time. That was a no-go.

She was already having a hard enough time not thinking about him and how utterly wretched she felt. The last thing she needed was extra reasons to think of him.

"So…" Shelby prompted when Jillian stepped out of the closet wearing something else. "You'd been spending *all* your time in the stables lately. With a certain someone."

"Rediscovering my love of riding," Jillian said. They both knew it was a lie.

Shelby snorted. "I think it's safe to assume that something has happened between you and Nick."

"That's a large assumption."

"Is it?" her sister said. "My sources tell me you've been hiding out in the house, which sounds to me like you're trying to avoid running into him."

"Who are your sources?" Jillian demanded, narrowing her eyes. She couldn't believe it. Who'd ratted her out besides Mama?

"I cannot reveal names," Shelby said, aiming for a teasing smile.

Jillian huffed at her sister. "It was Mrs. Pulaski, wasn't it?" That woman was a hot gossip, and Roxie never would have betrayed her like that.

Shelby laughed softly and waddled across the room to sit on the edge of Jillian's bed. She watched her sister sink down and dropped her hands to her hips. A wedding and a baby. She was so damn happy for Shelby, and yet so incredibly sad at the same time. For one foolish second, she'd actually thought she'd found a similar bit of happiness for herself. Her chin wobbled, and she bit her lip. She would not cry. *She would not!*

"Jilly," Shelby said, cocking her head and patting the space next to her.

Jillian crossed her arms, determined to hold it all in. She'd already done the uncontrollable bursts of tears thing and the ice cream and rom-com marathon. She'd given herself three days to wallow in a miserable pit, closed off behind her bedroom door, and then decided that was enough. Because she was frankly sick of being sad. However good or bad their relationship had been, she'd been grieving her dad for weeks, and the last thing she wanted was to be grieving the end of this relationship with Nick, too.

It wasn't fair.

She should have known better than to let her heart get tangled up while the rest of her life was such a mess. In truth, she hadn't even realized how tangled it was until Nick had pushed her away. But like, *really*? How many problems did she need? Heartbreak, heartache, new siblings, missing siblings…

"I'm sorry," Shelby whispered, and those words were what almost broke her.

"Why are you sorry?" Jillian said as a single tear slipped from her eyelashes. "You didn't do anything."

"I don't like to see you hurt, Jilly."

Jillian brushed the tear from her cheek and wandered over to the bed, sinking down beside her sister. "I don't even know what happened." It all felt like a whirlwind. Falling for Nick and Mandy, losing Nick and Mandy. She told Shelby about that day in the stables when Mandy got hurt and what Nick had said to her at the hospital. "I just… I wish I could go back and do things differently."

"Different how?" Shelby asked.

"Never agree to meet Nick, for one," Jillian huffed. If she'd let Madeline handle that, remaining in her little bubble, he never would have meant so much to her.

"I don't think you actually mean that," Shelby said thoughtfully.

"Well, what does it matter? Because I can't go back." Jillian shook her head. Would she have traded the heartache for never knowing Nick? Never knowing Mandy? "I just keep telling myself this doesn't have to be a big deal. All things considered, Nick was hardly even a blip on my radar."

"It doesn't always have to be a long, drawn-out love affair to mean something," Shelby reminded her. "I learned that firsthand."

"Yeah, well, maybe I fell too hard and fast. Maybe I was just looking for someone to distract me from the mess our family has been since Dad died. And Nick was…just there!" Even as she said the words, she knew they were a lie. They burned like acid on the tip of her tongue.

"He wasn't some convenient distraction," Shelby argued. "I saw the way you looked at him and Mandy. We *both* know how you felt about them."

"But if I keep telling myself he was, maybe it won't hurt as much," Jillian said, her voice growing thick. She rubbed the place between her eyes, trying to massage away the tension. "God, I just want to scrub Nick Slater from my mind."

Shelby smiled sadly. "Have you tried to talk to him again?"

"Yes," Jillian replied, folding her hands in her lap to keep them from shaking. She was losing control of the grief. It was slipping free, and she hated that. "I reached out to him that evening, to check on Mandy and see how she was doing. To see if they needed anything." Nick hadn't picked up the phone when she'd called. "He finally texted me back the next morning to tell me she was doing okay."

"And that was all?" Shelby said.

"Well, I asked if we could talk about things. It was very tense in the hospital, and I thought that maybe now that things had calmed down a bit we could have a different conversation, but he just said that nothing had changed." Jillian sighed. Her chest felt hollow, her heartbeat ringing out. "He obviously doesn't think there's anything left to talk about."

"Sounds to me like he's just scared," Shelby said, patting her tummy. "I can't even imagine all the things that are going to frighten me once this little boy is born. I'm sure

I'll be freaking out every time he falls down or scrapes his knee or cries. I'm already discovering that being a parent is going to be sort of terrifying."

"You're going to be a great mom," Jillian assured her. She reached over and squeezed her hand.

Shelby smiled. "I'm gonna do my best at any rate. But, what I mean is, I'm sure it's the same for Nick. He was sort of forced into this with Mandy. He didn't get a whole lot of time to prepare for all the feelings that come along with suddenly being responsible for this tiny human."

"I know that," Jillian said. She couldn't even imagine the pressure he felt to keep Mandy safe and happy. But that was exactly the point. In Nick's version of protecting Mandy, there was no room left for her.

"Maybe he just needs some more time," Shelby suggested. "To really let things settle. And once he feels a little more in control of the situation, you two will work things out."

Jillian's heart leapt at the thought, but she wasn't sure about that. Nick had sounded pretty sure of his decision in the hospital, and he hadn't budged when they'd texted. "He needs to focus on Mandy right now," she said. "That's what he told me, and I'm doing my best to accept that. And besides, I need to focus on helping the family figure out Dad's stuff." She nudged Shelby. "And sometime soon, I'm going to have to focus on being a really good aunt."

"I think there's a world where you can do all of those things," Shelby murmured.

"Nick doesn't seem to think so," Jillian replied sadly. And she just had to be okay with that.

After her talk with Shelby, Jillian drove downtown to Emerald Ridge Boulevard to meet Melissa and Rory for coffee. She walked into the Emerald Ridge Café, located in the town's most luxurious hotel, and stopped at the coffee bar to order herself a vanilla latte. Following a moment of deliberation, she bought the biggest, gooiest, fudgiest brownie from the pastry display case. She asked for a couple extra forks, but she honestly had no desire to share.

She was still masking her pain with copious amounts of ice cream and baked goods.

"Uh oh," Melissa said as Jillian made her way over to them. She winced. "Girl, you look rough."

"I feel rough," she admitted, slumping down in a chair. It was easier to be up-front with her friends. Part of her hadn't wanted to drag Shelby down with all her miserable thoughts while she was planning her wedding and prepping for the baby. But Melissa and Rory wanted the gossip. They were dying to know what had happened, and after she'd finished telling them, the brownie was gone, and Jillian was feeling slightly better.

Every time she told the story, it felt like she unraveled the twine that was strangling her heart. And with every mention of his name, she thought she might one day be able to get over Nick Slater. But today was not that day.

"So, are we allowed to hate him or what?" Melissa said.

"How can you hate a guy for breaking up with you to look after his niece?" Rory countered.

Jillian thumped against the back of her chair. That was the crux of her problem. She was horribly upset, and yet she couldn't even be mad at Nick. "I know what that little girl has been through," she said. "What she's *still* going through. I can't fault him for wanting to put her first. For wanting to protect her."

"Yeah," Melissa replied. "That's all well and good. We love a protective man. But it sorta feels like he didn't know what to do with his feelings, so he freaked out, found something to blame that he could control, and you got caught in the crossfire."

Jillian hummed. Who was she to judge him? She wasn't a parent. After listening to Shelby talk about how terrified she was to become a mom, Jillian really couldn't blame Nick for being upset that Mandy had been hurt or for how he'd handled it.

"It sounds to me like you were trying to comfort him," Rory said. "And to be a comfort to Mandy."

"I was." She thought she'd been helping in the moment but clearly not. "I was freaked out myself, but I was mostly trying not to upset Mandy more by having a big reaction."

"Exactly. You were only trying to help. So I think you're allowed to be a little mad at Nick," Melissa added. "That's all I'm saying."

"I'm not mad though," Jillian said. "I don't think there's a part of me that will ever be mad. I'm just…upset. And I miss them." Her jaw trembled. It had been doing that a lot lately. "I wasn't looking for Nick, but somehow I stumbled upon this little family of my own, and now it's just…gone."

"Would more cake help?" Rory asked, looking as miserable as Jillian felt. "Should I get cake?"

She huffed a humorless laugh. "I don't think there's enough cake in the world. Or ice cream. Or chocolate. Trust me, I've been trying." There wasn't enough of anything to fill the gaping holes left inside her in their absence. "I just… I want Nick."

Melissa sighed. "Well… If that's still how you feel, then I say, go for it."

"I *can't* just go for it," Jillian said. "If that option was on the table, I would have already followed that up. He doesn't want anything to do with me or us or a future together."

"Sure you can," Rory chimed in. "You just have to fight for him."

"He told me he was done," Jillian told her friends pointedly. "I don't know how to fight for that." Nick's heart was closed to her, and she'd been trying really hard not to draw comparisons to her absentee dad, but in a way, it felt like she'd been abandoned all over again. Like Nick had walked into her life and then walked out, leaving her wishing and waiting and wanting.

She didn't want to wait around for someone to care about her anymore.

"I just want someone to choose me," Jillian said. And despite everything, she wanted that someone to be Nick.

Rory's lips pulled into a thin line. "Maybe we can make him come to his senses?"

"Guys do tend to be a little slow with these things," Melissa said in agreement. "He might need a push in the right direction. Or more time to process."

"That's basically what Shelby said," Jillian told them. Disappointment and rejection created a nasty concoction in her belly. "You know, after everything I've been through with my dad, you'd think I would have known better than to actually trust anyone with my heart."

"That's not true, Jill," Rory said, getting up and coming to sit beside her. She leaned against her. "You have to keep your heart open. Maybe not for Nick, but for someone else to come along and choose you." She gestured to Melissa. "We chose you, didn't we?"

That got a smile out of Jillian.

"Yeah, unfortunately for you," Melissa joked, "you're stuck with us."

"But I'm serious," Rory said. "If you close your heart off, you might miss out on something wonderful."

Maybe Rory was right. In time it wouldn't feel so difficult to leave her heart open, to leave it exposed and vulnerable again. But until that time came, she needed to take her mind off of Nick and Mandy.

"I think for now I need to commit my heart to something other than love," Jillian stated. While wallowing, she'd had a lot of time to think about her life, and she'd come to the conclusion that she was ready to do something more meaningful with it—and honestly, something good had to come from all this heartache. "Remember how I told you guys about my dad's donation to the children's department at the hospital?"

They nodded in tandem.

"Well," Jillian continued, "I'm thinking of starting a costumed character charity at the hospital. Even without Dad's inheritance secured, I think I could still raise the funds to keep it going through my connections or different galas and events."

Melissa frowned. "A what?"

"Oh!" Rory said. "I *love* that idea. You know," she said to Melissa, "when someone dresses up as a superhero or whatever and visits the sick children?"

Melissa blinked. "That's…really cool, actually. How'd you come up with that?"

"Well, it was partly thanks to Mandy," Jillian explained, smiling sadly as she did. "The first time I met her, she called me a princess, and the nickname sort of stuck with her and Nick. And the other part was thanks to my dad. When I found out about his donation, everything just sort of clicked, and I realized what I wanted to spend my time doing." She'd never been certain of her path before—she'd actually started to think that maybe it included Nick—but either way, she knew this was what she was meant to do.

Now she could truly combine the joy she found volunteering with her love of acting. In a weird way, without meaning to, her dad had helped her figure out that much. She wanted to leave some good behind in this world. And what better way than by using her talents to make a sick child smile?

"Does this mean I get to dress up as a princess?" Melissa asked. "Because sign me the hell up."

"Agreed," Rory said. "I want the tiara and everything."

"And it's going to operate through the hospital?" Melissa wondered.

"I think so," Jillian said. "The gift shop in the lobby's been closed for months. I'm thinking of getting a proposal together and seeing if the board will rent the space to me."

"Ooo, what are we calling it?" Rory asked, tapping her chin.

Jillian grinned at their enthusiasm. "No idea. But I'm open to suggestions."

"Emerald Ridge Character Crew," Melissa threw out.

"That's *horrible*," Rory said.

"It is not!"

"How about ER Enchantment?" Rory said. "Or ER Heroes? The Magic Makers. Fairy Tale Crew?"

"Now you're just piggybacking off my name," Melissa complained.

Rory shook her head. "I've improved it."

Jillian laughed again, and her heart felt light for the first time in days. "The Fairy Tale Crew," she said, pondering the name. "I kind of like the sound of that."

Rory smiled, smug.

Mandy would have loved it, too. Jillian sighed. What a bittersweet thought.

Chapter Nineteen

Nick stared at himself in the bathroom mirror, running a hand over his stubbled jaw. He hadn't shaved for days, and Mandy was starting to look at him funny—sorta like he was a stranger. When she'd reached up and touched his cheek with her good hand this morning and whispered "ouch" at the scruff, Nick had decided enough was enough.

He had to pull himself together.

Because he didn't recognize himself right now, either.

He ran the water and lathered up his face with shaving cream, wondering how everything had gone so wrong.

He'd been happy with Jillian. So damn happy. But now there was a hole in his chest that hadn't been there before, an ache in his gut that wouldn't go away, and the world outside had been reduced to gray. Nick knew what the heartbreak of a relationship was—he'd been through it when Sylvia left him after his brother passed. Letting her go had been hard, but letting Jillian go… That, for some reason, felt infinitely worse. Nick didn't know how she'd wormed her way into his heart so quickly. Or so deeply. But she had. And now all he wanted was her smile, her laughter and her soft words whispered against his lips in the dark. He wanted her beside him in the stables in the morning while he did chores and across from him at the dinner table in the evenings.

He wanted her, even now. But it couldn't work.

She was a distraction he couldn't afford if he was going to do right by Mandy. He ran his razor under the water then shaved the scruff from his cheeks and chin. He tried to shave away the loneliness and grief, too. But that couldn't be cut away.

People said you knew when you'd found *the one*.

But they never prepared you for what it felt like to let go of that person. Now he was just trying to go through the motions every day. Wake up. Think of Jillian. Drop Mandy off at school. Think of Jillian. Chores. Think of Jillian. He'd been working himself hard these past few days, hoping that he'd fall into bed too exhausted to think about Jillian, but even when he was dead tired, she showed up in his dreams, that look on her face in the hospital haunting him right through to morning.

He didn't want to miss her this hard.

Or to worry Mandy.

That was why he needed to pull himself out of this funk of his own making. *He* was the one who'd ended things, who'd told her they were over, so he didn't get to wallow. Nick tapped his razor against the side of the sink, picked up a towel and cleaned the leftover shaving cream from his jaw.

Better, he thought as he looked in the mirror.

He looked like himself.

Now he just had to act like it.

Nick finished up and headed for the living room. He'd left Mandy watching one of her shows, but she'd moved from the couch to linger by the dining room window—the one that looked out over the porch. She'd pulled up a dining table chair and climbed onto it so she could stare out at the property, craning her neck to look down the path.

"Hey, Squeaks," Nick said, coming up behind her. "What are you looking for?"

She lifted a tiny finger to the glass. "Jillian?"

That one word was a punch in the gut.

He watched her press her forehead to the window, waiting for Jillian to appear. He felt horrible knowing she never would. But how did he explain that to a four-year-old?

"Come here," he said, scooping her gingerly into his arms. It had been days since Mandy had been injured, and in that time, she'd become his sole focus again. As he looked down at her now, her face expectant, her eyes wide, it felt like someone had carved out a space between his ribs and left the wound to fester, open and unable to heal.

Nick carried Mandy over to the couch and sat her down next to him. "We need to have a little talk, okay?"

Mandy cocked her head, her little blond eyebrows furrowing. He wanted to wipe away the lines of her confusion. "Remember when I told you a few days ago that Jillian was going to be spending time with some other friends now?"

Mandy nodded, her bottom lip sticking out in a pout.

"Well…" he sighed. How was he supposed to act like everything was fine when she was blinking up at him with that look on her face? "That means she's really, *really* busy."

"But she's coming over?" Mandy said.

Nick loved when she used her words. Any other day he'd be celebrating the fact that she'd strung together a sentence for him, but right now it felt like Mandy was digging at that hole in his chest, scraping and clawing. "She's not going to be coming over, Squeaks. Not anymore."

Mandy pursed her lips at him, her little face screwed up. He knew she was confused. But there was no way to explain heartbreak to her. She thumped her back against the couch, jostling her arm where it was still tied up in the sling around her neck. "I want her come over!"

"I know," Nick said hoarsely. He ran his hand over her head, her pigtails skewed. They were never as good as when Jillian had done them, and the sight made his stomach ache.

"We go see her?" Mandy asked.

Nick shook his head.

His niece scowled at him in a way that momentarily reminded Nick of his brother. It stirred longing inside him, just adding to the painful concoction already there.

"I'm sorry." It was all Nick could think to say. Because how did he even begin to make her understand that this was for the best? She obviously missed Jillian enough to use her words more than usual. To express her frustration. Trisha said she might start to do this—that big emotions would encourage her to talk. Nick just never expected it would be over this.

His heart crashed against his ribs. Jillian's warmth and kindness and sweet attention had helped pull Mandy out of her shell a little more with every day they spent together. When Sylvia had dumped him, Mandy hadn't known her, hadn't grown attached…hadn't *loved* her. But things were different with Jillian.

She'd very clearly wormed her way into Mandy's heart, too, and Nick was going to have to figure out how to fill that void until Mandy forgot about her. Because choosing this little girl, making her the priority, ensuring she was safe and content—he owed that much to his brother. This was the right choice for them both. "We can still have lots of fun today," Nick told her. "You and me."

Mandy gave him a little side-eye that made him laugh despite everything.

"We're gonna be okay, Squeaks." He tugged her close enough to drop a kiss to the top of her head. She squirmed in his arms. "'Cause it's you and me together forever. Got it?"

"What do you mean you don't want to play?" Nick asked as they pulled up at Emerald Ridge Park. "You love the park."

Mandy stared out the window of the truck, considering the scene with an unimpressed look on her face.

When Andrew had texted him earlier about taking the kids to the park, he had jumped at the idea, if only to give them both something to do other than think about Jillian. He'd been hesitant to let Mandy run around too much these past few days in case she bumped her arm again, but she hadn't been complaining of any pain, and as long as she was careful, he figured she could enjoy the sandbox at the playground. He'd brought along her sand toys—an assortment of shovels and buckets shaped like castle turrets—and they'd already talked about how the slides and bigger equipment were off-limits until she was out of the sling.

"Let's just go check it out," Nick said as he watched Andrew pull up in his van. His two youngest kids piled out and made a beeline for the playground. "Maybe you'll change your mind."

Mandy's expression was doubtful.

Nick got out and walked around the truck to unbuckle her from her car seat and grab her bag of sand toys. The park was located at the start of downtown, facing the beginning of the boulevard. It was filled with ornate benches, charming footbridges, a huge duck pond and the playground. He brought Mandy here last Christmas to watch the tree lighting. It really was one of her favorite places.

She held his hand through the parking lot, skipping a bit as they drew toward the green.

"Jillian coming?" Mandy asked him, sounding a little more enthusiastic than she'd been in the truck.

Nick blew out a breath. He should have seen that one coming. "No," he said softly. "But Andrew's here!" He pointed him out ahead. "And he brought Joel and Larissa for you to play with."

Mandy sighed, shuffling beside him as he led her over to the sandbox with her toys. She got settled, filling up one of her castle buckets with a little yellow shovel. Larissa came over to say hello. Joel was too busy roaring like a dinosaur at the top of the slide to notice.

Andrew was shaking his head, watching his son as Nick walked over. "Honestly, sometimes I don't know where that kid gets his energy."

Nick snorted. "What are you talking about? This is the same energy you give off running around the hospital with the kids. He's you in miniature." His eyes drifted back to Mandy. Larissa had run off to the playground and was waving at Mandy from the bridge. Mandy looked on as she called her name but didn't appear very interested.

"Kid looks like you let a horse stomp on her favorite stuffie," Andrew said.

"She thought Jillian would be here," Nick explained.

"Ah." His buddy rubbed at his chin, looking out at the kids. "Still no change there?"

"With the breakup?" Nick said. He gave a humorless laugh. "You do know how those work, don't you?"

"Just figured you might have broken down and talked to her."

"Nothing left to say," Nick grumbled.

Andrew nudged his shoulder. "I don't think that's true. You look as miserable as Mandy."

"Yeah, I thought the park might help," Nick said. They watched the kids for a beat. Joel and Larissa had made their way back to the sandbox. They tried to cajole Mandy into building a giant castle with them, but she just sat there. Her eyes drifted across the playground to another little girl playing alone with a doll.

"You know, I haven't seen you as happy as you'd been lately in…forever," Andrew said. "And I'd say that's thanks to Jillian. Just putting that out there."

"Yeah, well… I know where my focus needs to be right now." Nick nodded in his niece's direction. "And unfortunately, Jillian can't be in that picture. Not if I want to give Mandy all the attention she needs."

"Look, maybe you're right," Andrew said, "and this was the right choice. But—"

"I don't want to hear your *but*," Nick snapped. He removed his hat, ran his hand through his hair and replaced it.

"Don't care," Andrew said. "I'm gonna tell you anyway. Because with my wealth of experience, I'm qualified to tell you that raising kids is hard."

Nick frowned. What did that have to do with him and Jillian?

"There's no rule book," Andrew continued. "Kids get hurt, and it's scary as hell, but you shouldn't push away someone that truly cares about you *and* Mandy. It doesn't sound like Jillian meant any harm with her words."

Nick bit his cheek. He'd told Andrew what Jillian had said at the hospital. *No big deal… Kids bounce back.* He hadn't wanted to admit it, but those words had terrified him. Because what if it *was* a big deal one of these times? What if something happened that Mandy couldn't bounce back from? He'd already lost his brother, he couldn't bear anything happening to her, too. "Maybe not," Nick said. "But what does it matter now? She said what she said. And I said what I said."

"You reacted the way *any* scared parent would," Andrew insisted.

"What?"

"You reacted like any parent," his friend repeated. Nick must have looked stunned because Andrew laughed. "What? Did you not think you were a parent now? Hate to break it to you, man. But you're not just an uncle anymore. You're a full-fledged parent."

Realization hit Nick like a hay bale to the back. He almost felt like he needed to sit down. Was that why he was so tied up in his own thoughts and fears? Because he'd become a parent without realizing it, and when he'd faced his first big scary moment since losing his brother, he hadn't known what to do?

"And I can say with full confidence that it doesn't get any easier, no matter how old your kids get," Andrew said. "Having your heart walk around outside your body is terrifying. But sometimes, as a parent, it's nice to know someone else has your back."

As he said it, Joel flung sand at Larissa, and she burst into tears, shouting for Andrew. He sighed, giving Nick an encouraging smile before walking off to break up their fight.

Nick turned back to watch Mandy, processing the other man's words, and as he did, Mandy sucked in a giant breath, her cheeks puffed up. She quickly released it, her little nostrils flaring, exactly the way she'd once practiced with Jillian at the cabin when they were playing. Then, to Nick's surprise, she marched across the playground toward that little girl with the doll, opened her mouth and started talking to her. Nick blinked repeatedly at the sight, stunned. Mandy talked and she didn't stop, the two of them giggling together before long and running off to hide under the slide.

"Careful!" Nick called, reminding Mandy of her arm, but he was so pleased to see her making a friend that the rest of his warning died away. Elation and pride won out over the fear and the worry, and the only thing he wanted to do right now was call Jillian and share this moment with her.

With a sudden bout of clarity, he realized that she was right. Kids *were* resilient. And he wasn't going to be able to protect Mandy from every hurt or loss. He wanted her to feel loved and safe and supported, but by pushing Jillian away, *he* was the one who'd ended up hurting Mandy. He'd taken her words in the hospital all wrong, and as if to drive that point home, here Mandy was thriving all on her own. If he really loved Mandy, he'd want her to experience everything the world had to offer. He'd want that for himself, too. His heart crashed against his ribs as he realized just how badly he wanted Jillian in their lives now, tomorrow and every day to come. He didn't care that they came from different worlds, because in truth, he'd been the one clinging to those differences out of fear, all while ignoring the ways in which they were the same.

But it was time to trust that those similarities were stronger than those differences, because he loved her.

He *did*.

And that love was stronger than his fear of losing someone again. That love was strong enough to merge their worlds into something beautiful and better. His world was fuller with Jillian in it, and Nick wasn't ready to give up on them yet. He reached into his pocket for his phone, his hand trembling as he texted her. Can we talk?

He needed to make things right. Somehow, if he still could, if she still wanted him and Mandy, he needed to win back Jillian's heart.

Chapter Twenty

"Where is my phone?" Jillian complained. "I swear I can hear it buzzing in one of these boxes." She picked up a box, looking beneath it, narrowing her eyes as it kept buzzing then stopped.

Oh, well.

She'd find it eventually.

"Jill, where do you want this one?" Melissa asked as a mover wheeled in a large, metal filing cabinet on a dolly.

"Uh..." Jillian glanced around the space. Part of her still couldn't believe she was doing this. That the hospital board had actually approved her proposal and let her set up the charity in the old gift shop behind the patient information desk. Maintenance had been by to clean the place up, and it still had that fresh paint smell. She'd dipped into her savings to get them started, and The Fairy Tale Crew was officially a go. "Maybe behind the desk? What do you think, Mel?"

Melissa held her hands up, framing up the wall like a photographer. "I say you keep the files in the back and the fun stuff up front."

Fun stuff being the costumes. Jillian nodded and the mover wheeled the filing cabinet into the back corner of the space just as another showed up with more boxes labeled Costume Supplies. She'd been on an ordering spree, but even she didn't know what half this stuff was. When she'd gotten around to telling Shelby and her mother about her charity plan, they'd excitedly offered to contribute their shopping skills.

The mover placed a stack of boxes next to her, and Jillian opened the top one to find nothing but plastic tiaras. There were tall ones and short ones and ones with sparkly jewels and dangly bits and bobs.

"Oh, yes!" Melissa said, walking over and placing a tiara on her head. "Sign me up." She practiced a royal wave. "Now all I need is a prince to go with it."

Jillian smirked. "This is most definitely a Shelby contribution." She'd already offered up a bunch of her old pageant costumes as well.

Melissa dug through another box and found a hot pink gown to go with her tiara. "This place is going to be so cute once all the costumes are unpacked!"

"I better get those racks built," Jillian muttered, looking around for the right box, "so we have somewhere to start hanging all this stuff."

Melissa strung some costume jewelry around her neck. "We should totally get the charity on social media. You can bring awareness to different childhood illnesses. Do cute little get-ready-with-me segments. Set up donation links. There would be so many good outreach opportunities."

Jillian smirked. "You just want an excuse to get dressed up every day."

"If the position of social media manager is open," Melissa said, "I wouldn't be opposed."

"Well, then how could I ask anyone else?"

Melissa squealed and hugged her. "I can't wait! I'm gonna start filming content now. You know, all the behind-the-scenes stuff that everyone loves."

"Just make sure you get my good side," Jillian teased.

Melissa's phone buzzed. She dodged another mover and snatched it up. "That's probably Rory with the coffee." She frowned down at a message. "Mmm…"

"What?"

"SOS. Apparently she dumped the coffee all over her car. I better go out and help her."

Jillian pointed to a box. "There should be cleaning supplies in there. Feel free to take whatever."

"Thanks," Melissa said, grabbing a roll of paper towel from the box. She headed for the door while Jillian kept looking for the costume racks.

"We're not open quite yet," Melissa said suddenly.

Jillian glanced up to see that Melissa had planted herself in the doorway, arms crossed as she stared up at *Nick*.

"Jillian? There's a tall, dark and handsome cowboy here to see you," Melissa said. "Would you like me to send him in?"

Jillian's heart thudded. What on earth was Nick doing here? She ran her hand down her front, smoothing her blouse nervously. God, it was good to see him. And there, clinging to his leg, was Mandy, staring up at all the boxes with trepidation.

Her heart thumped even harder. She'd missed that sight.

"Well?" Melissa said, shooting her a covert grin over her shoulder.

All Jillian could manage was a nod.

"I'll just leave the two of you to…*talk* then," Melissa murmured dryly. "While I go rescue Rory." She adjusted the tiara on her head. "Probably should have found myself a cape instead." And then she slipped out the door, leaving them alone.

"Hi," Nick said. He tilted his head, looking past the chaos, and gave her half a smile.

"Hi," Jillian replied. There was so much more she wanted to say, but the words lodged in her throat.

"Princess!" Mandy cried excitedly, spotting the pink gown Melissa had unpacked earlier. She ran over to it, gathering the material with her free arm, her mouth open in awe as she tangled her fingers in the sequins.

Jillian picked up the box of tiaras and put it down next to Mandy.

She gasped. "*Princess!*" she cried even louder. She wrapped her arm around Jillian's legs, squealing excitedly. Jillian's heart clenched, and for a moment she thought she might burst into tears. She'd missed this little girl as much as she'd missed Nick.

He walked into the space, shifting his broad frame carefully so as not to knock anything over. He chuckled a bit as he reached her. "I tried calling you," he said.

Jillian bit her lip. "Haven't been able to find my phone for a while."

Nick nodded. "I hoped it was something like that and not that you were ignoring me. Though I probably deserve it."

"I wasn't ignoring you," Jillian said.

"Well, on the off chance you were, I swung by the ranch to talk to your sister, and she said you were here."

Jillian's pulse raced. He'd been looking for her? That was a good sign, right?

"She did not prepare me for all this," Nick said. "What even *is* all this?"

Jillian chuckled at his question even as her heart ached from missing him so much these past days. "I'm…starting a costumed character charity. You know, to cheer the kids up."

Nick's face split in amusement.

"What?" she asked, intrigued by the look.

"So what you're saying is that you're gonna put your acting chops to use and be an actual princess?" he clarified. "With the tiara and everything?"

Jillian snorted and shrugged. "I'm hopefully going to manage an entire team of princesses."

"Guess that makes you the queen," Nick mused.

Jillian couldn't help her smile.

Mandy pried the most glittery tiara out of the box. "Look!" she declared, showing them. "Pretty!"

"It is very pretty," Jillian agreed. She led Mandy over to a tall, rectangular mirror that leaned against the wall. "Let's try it on, huh?" She placed the tiara on the child's head, shifting her tiny blond bangs out of the way. "What do you think?"

Mandy examined herself in the mirror, then beamed. "I get one for Uncle Nick!" She raced back over to the box, inspecting her choices.

"Oh, goody," Nick said. "Just what I've always wanted. To trade my Stetson in for a tiara."

Jillian chuckled, and her heart yearned for him. She crossed her arms, trying to stamp down the emotions that surged to the surface. She couldn't want him like that. Not when she didn't even know why he was looking for her. "What are you doing here, Nick?" she asked while Mandy was occupied.

"I came… Well, we spent all morning at the park," he said. "And I realized a lot of things."

"Like what?"

"Well, the first thing I want to do is apologize."

"You do?" she asked, her hands trembling. She clenched them into fists.

"I was wrong," Nick said thickly. "About so many things. And you were right."

"That's not what it sounded like at the hospital," she said, that day flashing back like bursts of a nightmare.

Nick looked stricken. "I was out of my mind with worry, and I should have been leaning on you for support."

"I wasn't trying to get in the way of you being there for Mandy."

"I know that," he insisted. "What you said… I wasn't ready to hear it then. But you were trying to tell me the truth, and it took me until today to see that Mandy *is* resilient. And I realized I've been holding on too tight, trying to stop her from getting hurt, but in doing so, *I* was the one who hurt her."

Jillian nodded.

He reached out and brushed a loose strand of hair from her cheek. "I never should have pushed you away, Jillian."

She tried to say something, but she didn't even know where to start. The hurt in her chest ached despite how badly she wanted him.

"I'm sorry," he said, his voice softened, raw.

She blinked back the weight behind her eyes. "Thank you for saying that."

Nick's face fell. "Have I ruined everything?"

She looked up at him, feeling a sob bubble up in her gut. Had he? Could they get back to what they had?

"Please say I haven't," he begged, catching her hands in his, pulling her close.

She was suddenly overwhelmed by the scent of him, by the desire to fold into his arms, to sink into the strength of his embrace. "I don't know."

"Jillian?"

Her voice wavered. "I don't want to be hurt again, Nick."

"I know," he said. "Darlin', I *know.* And I promise, you won't be."

"How can you make that promise?"

"You've done nothing but make my life better from the moment I met you." He kissed her knuckles. "You've made Mandy's life better, too. And I don't want to run from love anymore. I don't want to be afraid of loving and losing, because not having you in my life was infinitely worse."

"You *love* me?" she said, breathless.

"I do, Jillian. So much! And I want to spend the rest of my life taking care of you. I know I don't have extravagant things to offer you—"

"I never wanted any of that," Jillian insisted. "I just wanted you. And Mandy."

"Then you have us," Nick said. "And all of Otto's slobbery goodness."

Jillian choked on another sob.

"Love you, too!" Mandy piped up, hardly looking up from her tiaras. She said it so casually that Jillian and Nick both burst into laughter.

"Just in case you were wondering about that," Nick added.

Jillian swallowed the emotion that swelled in her chest. "Well, I love you both, very much."

"I know I don't have a great track record as of right now," he admitted gruffly. "But I think I was afraid of losing you and of not being enough for Mandy, so it felt safer to push you away before either of us could be hurt. But that's not what was best for anyone. I see that now. And I swear that will never be the case again. Do you think you could ever forgive me?"

She already knew the answer. She'd known it the moment he'd walked through the door. Because she couldn't live the rest of her life with Archibald's rejection hanging over her head. If she wanted to experience love, if she wanted to make connections, if she wanted Nick and Mandy to be hers, then she had to be willing to open herself up.

She had to be willing to risk disappointment and fight for what she wanted.

She'd finally found her purpose.

And now she'd found her people. So, she had to reach for them and grab on with both hands. She wanted this little family to be hers, and that was worth risking everything. "Yes," she said.

The corner of his mouth flickered, his eyes glassy. "Good," he said, holding her hands tighter. "That's good. Because you're stuck with us now. Right, Mandy?"

"Yep!" she said again, probably totally oblivious to what she was saying.

"And when we Slaters decide we want something, we don't give up the fight. You're a part of our lives now and always."

"*Always?*" Emotion tangled in her throat, almost stealing the words, but she forced them out past a sob of joy. "I like the sound of that."

"Well, all right then," Nick said. He gave her a crooked smile, then reached into the box of costume jewelry next to them, pulled out a ring and got down on one knee.

Jillian gasped. It felt like her heart had stopped.

"Jillian Fortune, queen of princess costumes," Nick said, holding up the plastic silver ring. "Would you happen to have an opening for a king in your court?"

"Are you asking me what I think you're asking me?" she said, disbelief washing through her.

He took her hand, looking into her eyes. "I don't want to wait any longer. I want to start our lives together. I want to be there for the good times and the hard times, and I promise to do everything in my power to make you feel loved and cherished and wanted every day for the rest of our lives."

That was all she'd ever wanted. To *be* wanted. Jillian could feel the tears well in the corners of her eyes. She attempted to blink them away, but it was a losing battle.

"Will you marry me?" Nick said, his voice thick.

"Yes," she said, feeling tears slip freely down her cheeks. A laugh bubbled free. "*Yes!*"

Nick slipped that costume ring on her finger and stood, pulling her into his arms. Jillian sank into his embrace, happiness rushing through her like pure sunlight. She felt so giddy she could melt.

Mandy squealed in delight, running over to them. Nick scooped her up, too. She snatched Jillian's hand to stare at the ring, giggling. "Too big," Mandy declared.

Nick grinned at Jillian. "Oops. Must have got the sizing wrong."

All she could do was laugh and beam at the plastic ring on her finger. "I think it's perfect."

"Yeah?" he asked. "Not too gaudy?"

She shook her head. "Honestly, it's the nicest ring I've ever seen."

Nick's cheek twitched with a smirk.

"Now we happy ever after?" Mandy asked, repeating the line from the book Jillian knew Nick read to her every night.

"You bet, Squeaks," he said. "Now we get to live happily ever after."

Jillian grinned at them both. "Forever and ever."

Chapter Twenty-One

King galloped gracefully across the round paddock at the side of the stables, his luxurious mane dancing in the breeze.

Jillian walked out and leaned her arms against the fence. King whinnied in excitement, rushing over so she could give him a scratch. His black coat shimmered beneath her hand. "How's my boy?" she asked.

He chuffed in response, nuzzling at her, and Jillian laughed.

"I don't have any treats for you. I heard you had more than enough today." Mandy had come by the stables with Nick earlier, her pockets full of apple slices. She'd taken a special liking to King in recent weeks, and he'd apparently monopolized her treat stash. Jillian gave him a gentle little shove. "Go on. Enjoy your time. You'll be coming in soon enough."

King picked up his trot again. Nick had been busy bringing in all the horses from the pasture for the night, feeding and watering them and getting everyone settled.

King was the last, getting to spend a few extra minutes under the glorious sunset. Behind the horse, the sun hung low in the sky, painting the horizon in creams and golds and a sweet blush pink. Jillian didn't think she'd ever seen a more perfect sight. She inhaled deeply as the smell of sweet hay blew on the breeze, and contentment filled her. It had been a long, stressful road since losing her dad, and there were still answers to find in order to fulfill the terms of his will, but for the first time in a long time, she had faith that it would all work out. Because she'd carved out her own little piece of happiness with Nick and Mandy now, and she knew the man of her dreams would be there to support her, whatever the future brought.

Footsteps sounded behind her, and Jillian turned, spotting Nick in his dusty blue jeans and Stetson. He'd cleaned up a little, having thrown a dark button-up over his white T-shirt.

"Well, don't you look handsome, cowboy. What's the occasion?"

Nick adjusted his collar playfully and winked at her. "Can't a guy want to look good for his girl?"

Jillian hummed as he caught her in his arms, his hands smoothing over the small of her back. "You always look good."

"Figured I should look *extra* good."

"What for?"

"Reasons." A dimple appeared in his cheek.

Jillian had no idea what he was talking about, but in his arms, she really didn't care. "All finished up for the night?" She wanted to spend the rest of the evening wrapped up in Nick, letting him whisper in her ear about the rest of their lives that they had to spend together.

"King's the last one out," Nick said.

"Want me to grab him?"

He shook his head. "He looks like he's enjoying himself. Why not let him run a little longer?" He leaned in and kissed her. Jillian savored the moment and the fact that they could just do this now, whenever they wanted. Because he was her fiancé, and they had forever.

"Where's Mandy?" Jillian asked.

"She's hanging at the house with Shelby for a few minutes."

"Oh?" Jillian said, frowning as he smiled at her.

"There's something I wanted to ask you." He squeezed her hand.

"Is there?"

He nodded, stepping back, and suddenly it all made sense. The reason he'd asked her to hang out with him while he finished the chores for the night, his spiffy clothes, the fact that Mandy was with Shelby.

"Is this a redo?" she asked, chuckling softly as Nick sank down to one knee. Sunset painted the stables gold, and Jillian felt like they'd actually stepped into a fairy tale.

"You bet it is," he said, pulling out a small velvet box from his pocket. He popped it open, revealing a simple, stunning diamond ring. "I know it's not much—"

She cut him off, shaking her head. "Nick…" Emotion swelled inside her. "It's *perfect.* The first one was also perfect." She didn't need any big, fancy diamond. She only needed him. And this. Nick and Mandy and the horses, and their perfect little life on the ranch.

Nick popped the ring out. "I wanted it to be a ring fit for a queen."

"It is," she said. "Because you picked it for me."

"Mandy might have had some input, too," Nick admitted.

"Then even better," Jillian said, holding her hand out to him and wiggling her fingers eagerly.

"Oh, did you want something?" Nick teased.

She pouted playfully. "Just ask me already."

"Before you change your mind?" he joked.

"As if… You're stuck with me, Nick Slater. From now until forever. So you might as well get used to it."

"In that case…" he said. "Jillian Fortune, will you agree to marry me…*again*?"

"Yes." She nodded and laughed, blinking back tears of joy. She'd come a long way in a short time, and there was more to do in unraveling the mystery of her dad's land, but Nick and Mandy were her constants now, and she loved them more than anything. And however much she'd struggled to understand Archibald Fortune, she wanted to believe that maybe it was *his* doing that brought Nick and Mandy into her life.

For that, she would always be grateful to him.

"A thousand times yes," she breathed as Nick took her hand and slipped the ring on her finger.

"Perfect fit," Nick said, grinning up at her.

"You did good," Jillian agreed. "Mandy will be very impressed with your efforts."

"Well, I've got two women in my life to impress now." He climbed to his feet. "So I gotta start strong."

"That's a tall order," Jillian said, smiling as he pulled her into his arms. "Keeping two women happy."

"It is," Nick acknowledged. "But I'm gonna love every minute of it." He took her hand in his and wrapped his other arm around her waist. Then he stepped to the side, turning them in a slow circle beneath the peak of the stables.

And as they danced there, with the sun painting the world in creamsicle hues and King's whinny carrying on the wind, Jillian only had one thought: Fairy tales really did come true.

* * * * *